HOW THE SUN SHINES ON NOISE

Matthew Deshe Cashion

Livingston Press
University of West Alabama

copyright © 2004 Matthew Deshe Cashion
All rights reserved, including electronic text
ISBN 1-931982-37-6, library binding
ISBN 1-931982-38-4, trade paper

Library of Congress Control Number 2004093711

Printed on acid-free paper.

Printed in the United States of America,
Publishers Graphics

Hardcover binding by: Heckman Bindery

Typesetting and page layout: Gina Montarsi
Proofreading: Jenn Brown, Ariane Godfrey,
Tomeika Walker, Joe Taylor
Cover concept: Joe Taylor
Cover design: Gina Montarsi
Cover photo: Matthew Deshe Cashion

This is a work of fiction.
You know the rest: any resemblance
to persons living or dead is coincidental.

Livingston Press is part of The University of West Alabama,
and thereby has non-profit status.
Donations are tax-deductible:
brothers and sisters, we need 'em.

first edition
6 5 4 3 3 2 1

for my mother

HOW THE SUN SHINES ON NOISE

Concrete conquers the South like Sherman's fire. But below Savannah, when Highway 17 bleeds away from Interstate 95, you enter a funnel that pulls you through thick pine woods toward the smell of something primitive. The sky darkens. Pine tops splinter light. The wind shakes the shadows on the road. Smell salt and mud and rotting fish. A paper mill spreading tidal waves of shit. Scratch and try to breathe. Rusty tin boxes, nailed to shaved bark, collect sap for whiskey stills. Deep inside the woods, old-timers sit around barns and boilers, toeing the dirt, confessing allegiances to swamps. Deeper still, inside hot churches, hands and feet keep time with spirit chants. Hear the wail of a mother whose son killed himself because he could not come home and he could not stay away. Cough and scratch and try to breathe. The smell will soon grow too familiar to complain about. Pass a billboard promoting paradise: a brightly dressed couple waving from an ocean-lined golf course.

Creeks break the rhythm of the woods. The flatness deepens. The sky opens on the flat brown marsh, wet from two high tides a day. Flatness breeds stillness. No help from hills. Falling pinecones do not roll. Rainwater stands, forming mosquito farms. Nothing rolls, and you can't see anything above the obvious. Water winds around and through the marshes, giving and taking life. Ancient oak trees lean on the shores of creeks, cradling secrets.

Every few miles, a dead tree stands above the rest, limbs twisted like a dancer imitating deformity. Empty nests adorn treetops. Strangled oaks wear Spanish moss like gray dresses hanging from great-grandmothers. On certain trees, from certain angles in certain slants of light, the moss resembles families of squirrels who have hung themselves.

The flatness deepens, the creeks widen, and the marshes darken. The afternoon gives itself in spoonfuls to the dusk. Wide creeks wind deep and out of sight. A solitary man paddles his boat toward a distant bend. Squint into the sinking sun. Scratch. Try to breathe. Roll your window down. Search for a stray pocket of fresh air. Find the melody of that strange hymn you remember coming from your grandmother's rusted voice. Repeat random fragments from childhood prayers. Scratch. Try to breathe.

Oyster shells covered the parking lot, and palm trees bordered the doors; gold calligraphy centered on the doors read: "*Coastal Georgia Sun*, OUR family dedicated to yours." I wondered if anyone saw me through the blackened glass. I wondered if my nervousness was noticeable. Wondered this too often. It made me nervous. Went in anyway. Inside, three old ladies sat in the dusky light beneath an "Advertising" sign. They didn't seem to notice me. Noticed then that I often went unnoticed, and that I didn't mind it. Smelled their hairspray mixing with mildewed newspapers and wet ink. Three Teddy Roosevelt look-alikes hung in picture frames from faded paneling. Someone in the distance smoked a cigar. A lady in advertising said, "I like mine on a bed of rice."

Descended the wooden staircase in the corner, and landed in a basement. A single fluorescent light fixture hung from chains in the center of the room and jaundiced every face and piece of furniture. An elderly woman slouched at the nearest desk, gray eyes swimming in opposite directions behind thick bifocals. To my right, four desks faced a urine-colored wall, three of them occupied by good-postured workers: an energetic man in his early twenties, a stout man in his fifties, and a hyper woman in her forties. They talked too loudly into their phones and typed too quickly on their keyboards. Certificates hung above their desks. Above the hyper woman's desk was taped this bumper sticker: "Have you prayed for a law officer today?"

Stood in the center of the room, put my hands in my pockets and pulled them out again. No one noticed. Eased toward an office in the corner, kept my feet outside and stuck my head inside. A small man sat on a pillow, drawing squares and rectangles on a piece of paper. Didn't know what to say, or the tone to use, or when to interrupt, so I cleared my throat.

He raised a pair of small red eyes to me, staring intently for several seconds without speaking.

"You're Leo Gray," he said.

Nodded.

"You look tired. Bad trip?"

"Haven't slept."

"What's that?"

"Didn't sleep."

"This job will cure you of that. Go sit at that empty desk out there until I call you."

Went to the vacant desk. The workers on either side of me welcomed me by way of apologizing for being busy, promising to get acquainted over lunch one day in the coming week, though they'd have to check their calendars. Mark, city and county-commission beat, took time to confess his four-handicap; said he'd soon take me to The Club, and then laughed the laugh some people give as conversation halters. Mary Kay, crime beat and restaurant reviewer, said she'd show me the places to avoid, though I didn't know if she meant neighborhoods or restaurants, so I simply smiled and nodded, and then she laughed the same kind of laugh that Mark had laughed, though louder. They assumed I was a stranger to the county faced with the pleasant diversions of getting to know the area, and I didn't correct them.

Mark, like Beethoven, (I'd read) used his entire arms at his keyboard to deliver greater power. Mary Kay talked too loudly into her phone, voice pointed at my ear while she collected the crime blotter from a guy named Tank, flirting around the edges of her enthusiasm. Her telephone voice was louder and chirpier than her speaking voice. The eighty-something year-old *Coastal Life* Editor whined too loudly to her assistant about Myrtice Brooks, who had won another bridge tournament. The fossilized sports editor in the far corner mumbled loudly, though indecipherably, to the man I presumed to be the publisher—Big Dick Taylor—about the Braves. I could only see the back of Big Dick Taylor's head, but I knew it was the publisher's head, because I'd seen his picture in the lobby beside his father and grandfather's pictures. In the coming days I would learn not to expect much in the way of a relationship, or even a hello, because Big Dick only talked to Orville, the sports editor (every day), and to Hank Snow, the editor (when he had to), and to his son, Little Dick Taylor (in passing). Little Dick occupied the desk outside Hank Snow's office, editing Business and Religion, having recently graduated with honors from journalism school at the University of Georgia—the only school his father would pay for him to attend. A framed certificate above his desk advertised membership in the Society for News Design, and beside that was a framed photograph of his college fraternity, all of them dressed in ties beneath a banner of Greek letters I couldn't read.

Big Dick's head was a white the shade of a turnip root. A thin line of white hair circled his head like the seams on a baseball. From the front, which I would rarely see, his face resembled the features of a bassett hound, eyes drooped and lifeless from a lifetime of morning martinis. This was the drink he started with at ten a.m., (according to legend) after coming in at eight-thirty to throw away his mail and to talk to Orville about the Braves.

Mary Kay said, "Oh Tank, you're bad. You're awful." And laughed hysterically.

Mark said, "I know what you're saying, Buck. Privatizing waste management saves taxes. I agree completely. I have it word for word."

The only items on my desk were a calendar and a pencil. I picked up the pencil, started doodling over the first week of August, and tried to remember what Kate—my fiancé of six months—had told me on the phone late the night before. She had called my mother's at midnight to say she'd changed her mind—that she wouldn't be joining me after all, though it was all her idea that I leave my job as a graveyard toll booth attendant at the Charlotte airport to take a job that would contribute something to *community,* and where I could apply what I'd been learning from all the books I'd been reading in the dead silence inside my womb of a tollbooth, as she called it. I could live with my mother, she said until I found us a *quaint* place near the beach with a wraparound porch where we could entertain neighbors bringing wine and cheese. It was her idea.

I'd met her during my brief stint as a door-to-door fundraiser for an environmental watchdog group (feeling a longing to belong to something, I'd answered an ad posted on a laundromat bulletin board). Kate was the only person in that, my only week, to invite me inside. She sat me at her kitchen table, introduced herself, and told me she worked through a United Way agency as a specialist in communication disorders working to rehabilitate stroke victims. The strong-smelling mutt she said she'd rescued from the landfill lay between my feet, snout propped on my left foot. Then she leaned forward and asked me to tell her all about the cause I was fighting for.

Tried to start the long spiel my group leader said would turn five dollars into fifty dollars: "We're fighting the dirty practices of the 2,500 hog farmers in this state who have an average of 5,000 hogs who excrete an average of 25 tons of waste per day that runs off into our streams, lakes, and rivers, causing respiratory problems, and sometimes vomiting. Every year—"

"You're talking too fast," she said, touching my hand.

Apologized.

"Start over."

"It would take sixty years for the people of Charlotte to produce the waste that North Carolina hog farms produce in one year."

"I doubt it would take them that long," she said.

Looked at my clipboard, worried I misspoke.

"Let's start again," she said. "What's your name?"

"Leo."

"Leo what?"

"Gray."

"What is it you want, Leo Gray? Be direct."

"I'm trying to save the planet from hog shit."

"That's funny. How about a beer?"

She pulled two beers from the refrigerator, passed one to me, and pulled a checkbook from a drawer. I covered my lips with my beer bottle, pretending to sip from it long after it was empty.

She invited me back to dinner the following weekend, and a month later invited me to move in.

A failure at fundraising, I returned to my tollbooth and continued to read and reread The World's Great Thinkers—Rousseau's *Contract*, Hegel's *History*, Marx's *Manifesto*; Schopenhauer, Heidegger, Nietzsche—the Transcendentalists, the French poets, the Modernists, and the Beats. Felt lucky I didn't have to miss the night like those who must sleep through it to trudge through the day, half-blinded by the sun and the push of crowds. On a clear night in June, I stared into the sky and told myself to remember this moment in my life, when I was in the exact spot where I wanted to be, feeling the kind of clarity I'd read was reserved for monks like Thomas Merton. The only urgency I ever felt was a desire to share the calm. Inhaled the night sky and then went home to Kate, and let the sky fall out of me. There was nothing I wanted except for things to remain the same.

Then one August night over dinner she asked me out of the blue if I wouldn't ever want bigger things.

Dropped my fork and stared at an organic tomato, suddenly feeling paralyzed.

"You're not getting any younger," she said. "And the world is literally passing you by."

Didn't have an answer. Hadn't seen it coming. Or maybe I'd seen something coming, and chose to call it something else on that day or that night or that weekend when whatever I'd seen I quickly chose to see as something else. Didn't know what to say.

"Where's your ambition?" she said. "Your drive?"

Had never heard her use these words. Had never known I was lacking these things.

"You're scared," she said. "You're scared to leave that tollbooth to see if you could actually accomplish something."

Didn't think that was it, but I didn't say anything again.

"It's like you want to live in a bubble," she said. "I think you'd stay there forever."

My head wasn't clear anymore. A ringing started in some distant corner of my brain—the same ringing that appeared in grade school when the pitch of teachers' voices matched the sound of bad brakes on distant cars. The ringing rose whenever a crisis cropped up and stared at me, begging for reaction.

"Maybe it's selfishness," she said. "And to be direct, I don't think I can invest a lot more time in someone who isn't interested in development."

Stared at my red leaf lettuce. *Invest.* She paused long enough for me to respond, but nothing came to me.

"Well?" she said.

Lifted my eyes from a piece of lettuce and stared at her. Opened my mouth and closed it.

"I want a family," she said. "I've been thinking it'd be nice to start a family in a quiet town beside the ocean—maybe your old hometown in Georgia. Isn't it real pretty there—and quiet? It's a small enough town—it must be real quiet. And we could get inside a network of people who help the community. I've already looked on-line for you a job. I'm sure you could stay with your mother for a week or two until you find us a place, and then I'll join you as soon as I close the house. I saw this newspaper job that would probably be good for you."

Stared at my red-leaf lettuce. "No—I don't have any—no—"

"How hard could it be? It's a small town. And you could end up doing some good—contributing, for a change—providing helpful information."

Cleared my throat for several seconds, and lifted my finger. "Information," I said slowly, "is not knowledge."

"I've already called the editor for you," she said.

"The truth," I said more slowly, "cannot be quoted."

"I set up a phone interview for this Sunday at nine a.m."

The ringing in my head scratched the backs of my eyes. "Nine a.m. in the morning?"

"That's redundant," she said. "Nine a.m. is always in the morning."

Fingered pieces of red-leaf lettuce, and stared at the ringing in my head. Occurred to me that I knew nothing. Occurred to me that Kate alone owned instructions on how to live a life, and that I should follow them to keep from losing her.

The editor called at 8:45, asking about experience.

"I have no—"

"We need a go-getter," he said. "Are you a go-getter?"

A bile-colored river swallowed the word *go-getter.*

"Can you start tomorrow?" he said. "We need a warm body."

Covered the mouthpiece, and whispered "tomorrow" for Kate in a tone meant as a question. She smiled and nodded.

"Are you there?" the editor said. "Can you start tomorrow?"

"Okay," I said.

"We'll see you at 0 eight hundred," he said, and then hung up.

Kate hugged me then—too long, I realize now—and talked of how wonderful our new lives would be. Left that afternoon, taking only clothes.

Then she called at midnight to say she wasn't coming. She talked of some client she loved and couldn't leave—a stroke victim in his sixties struggling to relearn the alphabet.

"I didn't realize how much he needed me," she said.

Wanted to tell her I needed her worse, but I didn't say anything.

She apologized between sobs, said she hated how she felt. Said the guilt would kill her. I wrapped the cord around my hands, saying nothing. She really thought she could leave, she said, until she realized how helpless he was.

"He's just like you," she'd said. "Or at least how you were, mostly. So afraid and tentative and unsure about everything."

I giggled to produce any sound at all. Wanted to say I needed her worse. Listened to her cry and mumble incoherently, until, apologizing, she hung up. Listened to the dial tone, and imagined a hospital machine that hums after someone's heart has stopped.

Deep into my sleepless night, I began to understand that I'd only been a project—someone to save in the fashion of stray dogs and men who shit themselves. It occurred to me that she'd arranged my relocation so my mother could nurse my broken heart. But I didn't want to be stuck here, back in the place I'd fled the same night I graduated high school. Stuck with twelve dollars crumpled in my front jeans pocket and a beat up truck that would soon break down. Stuck in the tiny house I grew up in, sleeping on the living room loveseat, listening to my mother cough from down the hall. It was Kate's money that was going to set us up. But now she wasn't coming. And I was stuck.

Now, on my desktop calendar, I doodled over August days, blackening the first week's numbers.

Mary Kay said, "Tank, you're just plain naughty." And laughed.

Mark said, "Buck, your handicap is your swing," and laughed.

My phone rang and startled me. Picked up the console and searched for a switch that would cause it to ring less violently. It rang four times while I held it in the air. Then I thought it might be Kate, calling to apologize, to say my fears were irrational and that everything would always be all right. I rehearsed a detached tone, professional and objective, to hide my desperation.

"*Coastal Georgia Sun,*" I said. "Leo Gray speaking."

"If you look into that little window on your phone, you'll see it'll say, 'Hank Snow calling,' and then you won't have to say, '*Coastal Georgia Sun,* Leo Gray speaking' every time. You want me to call back so you can try again?"

"I think I've got it."

"Lester, our photographer, is taking you to do a story on Sandy the Sand Dollar, the new mascot for the Chamber of Commerce. Give me twelve inches in ninety minutes." When he hung up, the photographer was ambling toward my desk, carrying a full cup of coffee and a camouflaged-colored camera bag. He wore dirty jeans, a white t-shirt, and a leather necklace that held a plastic PRESS badge.

He said, "Let's hit it."

He drove slowly down Gloucester Street, past banks, office buildings, car dealerships, and flapping flags. The cracked muffler on his truck made talking difficult, but I didn't mind. His truck felt like a bus, and it gave me the sick feeling that it was a school morning twenty years earlier. Looked out the window like I looked out the window then, feeling like a hostage being pulled through a foreign landscape. We passed a new hospital, a new travel agency, and a new hotel. The sun's glare bounced off the sides of buildings and pierced my eyes. He stopped at every yellow light.

"I almost didn't come in this morning," he screamed, "but if I don't come in, we got no pictures, and if we got no pictures, we got no paper. That place would fall apart without me."

Nodded, and looked at City Hall, the only building, at three stories, that could host aspiring suicides.

"Then they'd be thirty thousand pissed off people out there," Lester yelled, "not knowing what the hell was going on, you know? It's an important job. Me and you, we have important jobs."

Nodded, and looked at someone on a ladder changing prices for pounds of shrimp.

He asked me something I had to ask him to repeat.

"I said have you got you a woman?" he said.

Didn't want to tell him. Didn't want to hear myself say that it was true. Then remembered how Kate had taught me the health of revealing hurtful things. Keep wounds from festering, she said, by giving them a voice, where perspective can be gained, distortions minimized, and bitterness avoided.

"My fiancé," I yelled. "Sounds like she wants to break it off."

Lester stopped at another yellow light. "What you mean *sounds like?* You have to be more pacific than that."

"More what?"

"Pacific. You have to be more pacific. What'd she say?"

"She said she's in love with one of her clients—a paraplegic—and doesn't think she can leave him."

"Fucking-A," Lester said. "I don't know what to say to that."

It was a mistake to open up. Imagined Lester reporting my confession to the gossips in the break room, news of the new loner spreading within the hour.

Lester said, "You ought to come worship with us this Sunday."

Wanted to tell him I was an atheist, or that I was baptized into some satanic cult, though the simpler truth was that I no longer believed in groups.

"I play bass and my wife plays drums. We keep the whole thing together."

Nodded. Watched an old man leave the Salvation Army, pulling a price tag from a new sports coat. We passed another new travel agency and hotel and then the newly refurbished Victorian that housed the Chamber of Commerce, bordered with new palms, then pulled onto the shoulder of Highway 17, fifty yards from a woman in a yellow outfit who was waving wildly in our direction.

"Hell," Lester said. "Maybe she's single."

She wore yellow and orange striped stockings, colors slanted like a barber's pole. The stockings disappeared mid-thigh into an inflated smiley-face sun that stopped beneath her chin. She looked like a long-limbed reptile trying to shed its egg. She was on us before I had both feet on the ground. She held out a long yellow arm for shaking.

"I'm Sandy," she told us.

She wore strong perfume.

Lester said, "I'm Lester. *Chief* photographer of *The Coastal Georgia Sun*, and this here's Leo Gray."

Held my hand on my forehead like a visor so I could see the woman wearing the sun. She wanted to know if we didn't think it was a beautiful morning. Lester agreed it was. Behind us was the marsh, and beyond the marsh was St. Simons Island. At an adjacent angle in front of us, two smokestacks from the paper mill spewed grey-black smoke toward my mother's house. The smell of the mill swirled with the smell of the rotting marsh, and mosquitoes swam around my eyes. The mosquitoes had been one of the pleasures of leaving. They hatched in shallow water by the thousands and fed on flesh with teeth the size of razorblades. Built nests inside the hair and crawled inside your head. Swam on your face and fell into your eyes. Collected and deposited disease.

Sandy lifted her heels and waved tiny circles toward some kids in a Lexus minivan. Lester crouched fifteen yards away, camouflaged camera bag at his feet.

Tried to determine if she too was miserable standing beneath the sun, but her eyes were moving over all the moving cars, and when she looked back at me, I felt like she didn't see me at all. Wondered if her enthusiasm was real, or if it was something she cultivated because she desperately needed work—like a department store Santa. Wondered if she got through her days by overindulging in morning medications. If so, I envied her her pharmacist.

She waved at a Range Rover turning toward the island.

I said, "Do you mind if I ask you a question?"

She laughed at this. Touched my shoulder and said to go ahead.

Her peculiar perfume produced in me some strong memory of childhood misery. I took a backwards step toward the marsh, and batted gnats.

"Isn't it too hot for this?"

"I love it," she said. "It feels like I've finally made it to varsity cheerleading. Oh, but don't write that—don't say I never made it to varsity cheerleading. I'd be embarrassed. You promise you won't write that?" She touched my shoulder again.

"Okay," I said. "Sure."

She smelled like lemons and ammonia. It hit me then that her perfume was not perfume, but a homemade mosquito repellent similar to what my mother once made for me. I'd often spent entire afternoons wandering in the woods (playing a game where I tried to get lost), and after the first time I came home with welts all over me, my mother developed her mosquito repellent recipe, mixing household ingredients into a bowl she'd then smear over my arms and legs and face.

"Plus," Sandy said, "this *is* a beautiful place. I like living here, and I like informing other people what we have to offer." She waved at a U-haul turning toward St. Simons. "Our quality of life is beautifully defined by the natural environment of our coastal community," she said, waving a palm across the marsh. "And although we are known for our natural and cultural riches, it's the spiritual strength of our many communities that forms our foundation. We have more than 140 churches here to serve our residents, and many of our congregations can be traced to the last century, including Christ Church, which was founded in 1820." She waved at a florist's van turning toward the island and stepped still closer to me. "People come from all over to live here," she said. "Convenient beach access makes living here a breeze. Come coast awhile."

She smelled like my childhood summers. I stepped backward toward the marsh. Started sweating from the forehead. Kept my head low in case someone from my past drove by and recognized me and believed the only reason I was back home was because I had failed in the place where I'd been before. I planned to ask Hank Snow to leave off all my bylines. I cared nothing about seeing my name in print. Sandy stepped toward me and brushed her fat sun against my arm. She smelled like lemon-fresh Pledge mixed with rubbing alcohol.

Lester yelled, "Hey, Clark Kent, get out the picture."

The backs of my shoes sank in marsh mud. Marsh grass brushed my pants. The smell of rotting corpses came to me from below and behind.

She waved at a tractor-trailer hauling pine stumps, pumped her arm in the fashion of kids begging for the horn, and the driver twice answered her. Again, she stepped toward me, bringing the smell of garlic. I looked through her lightly coated Raybans and saw something disturbing in her eyes—the kind of misplaced conviction locked inside the eyes of the occult.

"Getting this job was all part of God's plan," she said. "It gets hot sometimes, and my feet get tired sometimes, but I wouldn't trade it."

Another florist's van turned toward the island and Sandy trailed it with her waving arm. A drop of sweat hung from the end of my nose.

"It's an important job," she said. "You know how much money tourism brings every year?"

"How much?"

"Lots," she said. "It's the number one industry. Except it's not the tourism industry anymore. It's the hospitality industry. They say for every dollar a tourist spends, it means about seven dollars for us."

"How much do they pay you?" I said.

"Don't answer that," Lester yelled. "That's nobody's business but your own, sweetie. Don't mind him. He's new."

Sandy shrugged and waved at another tractor-trailer loaded down with pines.

"I'd do it for almost free," she said. "I think this is a wonderful place to live. Cone County contains surplus amounts of health and beauty for next to no cost at all. Not only do we offer a dreamlike getaway, but also a sense of community and permanence. Whether you are in the market for a quaint cottage, a stylish condominium, or a historic residence, you will find the perfect home within our beautiful boundaries. We have 216 holes of golf, award-winning schools with dedicated teachers, and friendly real-estate brokers who will bend over backwards to find your affordable dream house."

Lester loaded a new roll of film and moved to Sandy's other side.

She smelled of mildew, and my mother's ancient kitchen.

Took another backwards step into the marsh and batted gnats. Saw a small fiddler crab slip sideways into the hole he called his home. The sweat ball fell from my nose. Sandy waved at a construction crew packed in the back of a truck, hats pulled over dour faces. One man lifted his hand over the tailgate and, without changing expressions, gave her the finger.

"I don't let things like that bother me," Sandy said. "All I can do is smile and say a quick prayer for that person."

The yellow makeup on her face was starting to undo itself from sweat. She smiled, and revealed a bottom row of yellow teeth.

"See that oak tree over there," she said.

Looked toward a bronze plaque that was planted next to a tree.

"That's where Sidney Lanier wrote his famous poem about our marshes."

Looked over the stinking marsh full of dull brown weeds where dead things hid, and remembered the poem I'd been forced to read in seventh grade—a rambling and romantic thing only a visitor could invent.

"Glooms of the live oaks," Sandy recited. "Beautiful-braiden and woven with intricate vines of myriad cloven."

Thought of the French poets I'd read in my tollbooth. *One evening, I sat*

Beauty on my knees. And found her bitter. This, from Rimbaud or Baudelaire, though I couldn't at the moment remember which. Sandy spread her arm across the marsh, palm up, and recited another line.

"When lovers pace timidly down through the green colonnades of the dim sweet woods, of the dear dark woods, of the heavenly woods and glades—"

I fled. O Sorceresses, O misery, O hate, to you has my treasure been committed. The poem in my head was from Rimbaud's *A Season in Hell* or Baudelaire's *Flowers of Evil*, though I couldn't be sure which.

"O braided dusks of the oak and woven shades of the vine, While the riotous noon-day sun the June-day long did shine Ye held me fast in your heart and I held you fast in mine."

Or was it Baudelaire's *Season in Hell* and Rimbaud's *Flowers of Evil?* Was already forgetting things. Wondered how quickly I'd forget everything I'd read.

"I will fly in the greatness of God as the marsh-hen flies in the freedom that fills all the space 'twixt the marsh and the skies," she said.

Backward the drowned go dreaming by. Wasn't sure anymore that it was Rimbaud or Baudelaire.

"By so many roots as the marsh-grass sends in the sod I will heartily lay me a-hold on the greatness of God."

I called to the executioners so that, while dying, I might gnaw the butt-ends of their rifles. Wasn't sure anymore that the poet was non-American.

"Look how the grace of the sea doth go," she sang.

And Spring brought me the idiot's hideous laughter. But who said that?

"About and about through the intricate channels that flow."

We exhale excrement. Maybe an American expatriate?

"We're lucky to live here," Sandy said.

*'You will remain a hyena' cried out the demon who crowned me with...*but I couldn't remember the rest.

Sandy yelled to Lester: "How am I doing?"

"You need to smile toward me, sweetie. Not *at* me. *Toward* me. That's it."

Sandy said, "He's really good, isn't he?"

She stepped closer and elaborated on how she loved her job. I smelled fabric softener mixed with Chlorine. She never took a lunch break she loved it so much. Without her work, she wouldn't know what to do, she said. The only people in her life, she confided to me, were the people she waved to, and her cat, Magnolia, without whom she might be lonesome. She spent her off-hours resting, preparing to work again. Today, after she clocked out at six, she planned to go home to her studio apartment (walking distance to the beach), eat a take-out shrimp dinner from The Crab Trap, slip into her pajamas and curl up with Magnolia to watch the colorized version of *Casablanca* (8:05 p.m., TBS).

"Lift your chin, sweetie," Lester yelled. "That's it. But don't look at me. That's it. Pretend I'm not here. That's it."

She waved at another florist's van turning toward the island. I batted gnats and wiped my forehead with my sleeve.

"That's a wrap," Lester said.

"I want to give you my beeper number," Sandy said to me. She reached inside her inflated yellow bosom, removed a business card and a pen, wrote a number on the back of it, and pressed the card into my palm.

She smelled like potpourri and gasoline.

Noticed then that she was wearing flip-flops, that her toenails were painted orange, that her toes were long and remarkably symmetrical, and on her left foot, on the toe next to the big one, she wore a silver ring.

"I think you're a nice person," she said. "I appreciate you taking me so seriously. Some people don't. We should get together and talk some more, sometime when we're not working and we can let our hair down, so to speak."

Thought the toe ring sexy. I liked her feet. I moved my eyes from her pretty toes, up her striped stockings, over her egg-shaped yellow sun, and holding my hand over my eyes, stared at the strange thing swimming in the center of her pupils.

"I mean it," she said. She grabbed my arm and held it. "I could cook for us. My place is right on the beach. Do you like long walks on the beach?"

Looked at her feet and nodded.

"Me too," she said. She walked me back to Lester's truck and closed my door for me, staring through the glass into my eyes. Lester pulled away, and she rotated her body in the direction of our leaving, waving a full-armed wave from tiptoes.

2

Wrote a ten-inch story in thirty minutes and sent it to Hank Snow the way Mary Kay instructed me. She and Mark had been blurring by me, rushing to Hank Snow's office and back again, yelling of jumps and column inches. Pockets of fat jiggled as they ran with copy to the production room, bringing back dummy sheets to recheck corrections, and then sprinting back to the production room before they could finally sit and breathe deeply, having met the challenge of getting yesterday's news off on time again.

Opened a new document and started a resignation letter.

Mary Kay opened a bag of chocolate chip cookies and surfed the net.

Listened to the overhead buzz of fluorescent lights. Spent a half hour writing, deleting, and rewriting my first sentence:

Dear editor: I'd like to exhaust my life inside a soundproof room, reading how the deaf have thanked their gods.

Then deleted it.

Mark swiveled his chair to face me, propped his forearms on his legs and asked if I was yet online. He made the quick gestures of someone cresting on a coffee buzz. He blinked rapidly and moved his eyes from side to side and nodded almost constantly. Shook my head. Didn't own a computer. Had never been on the Internet. Had heard it talked about, of course, but had so far been able to dodge a direct link to an internet-related conversation. When I pictured the Internet, I pictured myself lost inside a landfill. Mark stared at me gape-mouthed, full of pity.

Mary Kay talked into my other ear. "You need to get online," she said, and smiled the smile of children with new toys. "It's an invaluable journalistic tool for us. Information is a wonderful thing, isn't it? Of course they're still getting the kinks out. We lose our connection every time it rains." She straightened her posture and refaced her computer.

Smiled and nodded. Said I'd get online.

Mark yelled across me to Mary Kay, asking if she'd gotten the last joke he'd sent, and she answered yes, laughing, and said she'd sent it to Hank Snow and Little Dick. Mark picked up his ringing phone and confirmed a tee-time with a commissioner.

Started a new resignation letter. Spent another half hour writing, deleting, and rewriting my first sentence:

Dear editor: If being locked inside a sound-proof room is too ambitious, I'd like to revisit the silence of the late-night tollbooth, where a focus on futility can reach levels of clarity that border on the Buddhist ideal of needing nothing, a state which can then approach the Kantian Sublime.

Then deleted it.

My ringing phone said, "Hank Snow calling."

"This article is crap, Gray. You missed the story. Nobody wants to hear about how tired she gets, or about how she's all alone except for her cat, or how she gets the finger from construction workers, or how she still regrets not making it to varsity cheerleading. The story here is her commitment to community. And your paragraphs are the size of Russian novels. We'll bump this for today. I didn't know you'd be so green. Spend the rest of the day working on this. Get some practice. I have a bird-watching column we can run in its place. I spotted a pair of Brown Thrashers over on Jekyll Island Saturday, highly uncharacteristic for August." Then hung up.

Heavy machinery ignited in the recesses of the building and a high-pitched ringing bounced across the basement of my skull like thrown wind chimes. Plugged my right ear with a finger, but it didn't help. Three phones rang in the distance, each with a differently programmed sound. Tilted my head to dump the ringing. My eyes traveled outside my head, and looked back at me, unfocused. From where my eyes had traveled, my body resembled a heavy bag of garbage.

My headache fed itself. Every sound became a dart. Fluorescent lights buzzed above. Mark laughed with a commissioner the kind of laugh you hear from drunks. Mary Kay crunched chocolate chip cookies with an open mouth. Cigarette smoke swam in clouds from the break room down the hall. The vent above me was clogged with dust so thick it looked like moss.

Turned to Mary Kay; said, "Can you smell that?"

"I can't smell anything," she said.

"Is your nose clogged?"

"I just can't smell. Ever since I was little." She lifted her eyebrows as if to say she wasn't qualified to comment further, which meant it was a story she wasn't interested in pursuing. She offered me her bag of cookies. Waved them away and faced my blank computer screen.

Spent the rest of the morning slumped at my desk, absorbing all the laughter in the building. Little Dick Taylor laughed into his phone the laugh you hear from fraternity brothers preserving nostalgia. Mary Kay laughed with a cop the sick laugh that follows jokes of incest. Orville made apologies for the Braves to a loud janitor and they shared the kind of laugh that announced their hearts couldn't possibly take another one. Doris laughed with her assistant, Eula, the laugh you hear from old ladies criticizing mismatched marriages over cups of tea. A woman upstairs—probably in advertising—laughed the kind of violent laugh you hear from people who are whispered slander. Then Lester laughed the laugh of people who are in the know. Pictured my head as a dryer tossing jackhammers.

Spent the afternoon making telephones stop ringing. Took messages and placed them on proper desks. Forgot details. Times of calls and the times callers would next be available and the line next to the letters "re." Sometimes wrote wrong numbers. Mark and Mary Kay returned late afternoon, asking for the filling in of blanks. Voices like high-performance engines.

"I'm not a secretary," I said, even if my back was turned and slumped and my head was bent to my desk and my mouth was nearly closed. "I'm not going to be here very long at all," I told them, to myself.

3

The August heat of South Georgia (if you don't live on one of the islands and pay for ocean breeze) makes you feel as though you're wading through a swamp while wrapped in insulation. The air is heavy. You have to push yourself through it. It will steal your breath and swell your tongue and send you spiraling slowly into madness. So I bought a cold twelve pack at a convenience store and popped my first as I headed home.

Lacking air conditioning, rode with windows down. The pungent odor of the paper mill was thicker than I remembered—heavy as a phantom limb. All the businesses I'd remembered as a child were now failing, each of them linked to the next as if with a crooked spine. "Styles of London," was dark and empty—boards and trash strewn on top of amputated barber chairs. Propped against the inside window of "Coastal Computer Engineers" were three car tires. Cars with smashed windshields and missing hoods filled a fenced car lot in front of a miniature mobile labeled as "The Credit Doctor." Two men in overalls sat on either side of an oak stump they used as a coffee table. And on the corner, what was once a gas station, was now "Christ's Church for the End Times." A black iron fence enclosed a government-housing complex for the next three blocks. The fence surrounded three yellow-bricked buildings, the space between them occupied by dirt and metal clotheslines. Two women sat in kitchen chairs on the square slab of concrete that served as their front porch, clapping and laughing at an infant who danced circles at their feet. Green and yellow shotgun houses lined the next two blocks, yards shaved twenty feet by right-of-way easements. Tin-roof porches hung like the crooked bills of caps, and people sat beneath them, watching me pass. They sat beneath the falling odor of the paper mill, and fanned themselves with newspapers. Left their front and back doors opened and prayed for breeze. Porches packed with appliances and potted plants. Houses packed so tightly their meter boxes appeared to touch. Houses built overnight for the shipbuilders of the Second World War, painted in lead, insulated in asbestos, and regarded with resentment ever since. Plywood floors half-hidden by secondhand rugs, yard sale furniture, and ancient sinks spewing rust and air. Sounds amplified by bad acoustics: fathers stomping dirt from work boots on wooden steps; mothers clanking in tiny kitchens over fathers cursing because they couldn't hear their televisions over the clanking and the noise of machines inside their heads.

There was nothing to distinguish my duplex from the duplexes around us except for the fixture of E.B. Miller, the ninety year-old black man camped in his wheelchair outside his door, two feet from mother's door. We had no porch, and no grass, and almost no yard. We had two pieces of plywood joined end to end, indented slightly into the earth in front of our respective doors. Our view consisted of—ten feet away, and slightly above us—four lanes of traffic funneling people more efficiently now toward the islands; a constant gushing sound like crashing waves. To our right, we could see the top half of the mill's smokestacks. Across the four lanes of traffic there were duplexes like ours, though they seemed to be sinking too.

Put a beer in E. B.'s hand and sat in Mother's metal rocking chair next to him.

"What took so long?" he said. He popped the top, gulped greedily and moaned.

Dropped my head against the back of the chair, gulped my beer and dropped the empty can. Sweat leaked from my face and chest and ran down the insides of my legs. Rivers of smoke spewed into gray clouds and bled back out again.

E.B. had lived in the same spot since 1944, when he moved from Ohio to work in the shipyard, and though he'd worked a lot of jobs since then, all of my memories had him old and wheelchair-bound.

"Ain't the coldest beer in the world," he said. "But I reckon it'll do."

"I reckon it'll have to," I said.

E.B. wore the rectangular doctor-prescribed sunglasses his wife wore before she died. They stayed on the tip of his nose and hid most of his shrunken face. He'd been half-blind since the age of ten, when he crawled beneath a chicken coop and caught a nail in the eye, but he declared it a blessing—that it cut in half the ugly world. He lost his legs in 1964, when he was pinned against the mill's loading dock by a tractor-trailer picking up rolls of paper. The white driver claimed blind spots and bad signals. E.B. was compensated with a free double amputation at the knees, a wheelchair, and a pint of whiskey. Log splitters and oyster shuckers had pinched off three of his fingers. The skin on his left arm, from wrist to elbow, hung loose from being fried inside a deep-fry vat in the kitchen of the Cloister on Sea Island. He'd slipped on a shrimp, carrying a stack of bowls, and his arm went flying into sizzling grease. He spent his days now, sitting in his wheelchair, smoking his pipe, and staring at passing cars.

"That mill is killing people," he said. "They been turning up the stink late at night and on the weekends, when they think nobody notice. They got more orders from overseas, see, from places like Israel, so they got to crank up the stink and get that shit over there to them places." He stopped to relight his pipe.

Nodded to E.B., though I was on his blind side and he couldn't see. Smelled the mill and then smelled E.B.'s pipe on top of it. Something like cooked peaches. Thought then of Kate, and how I'd gone a whole half hour without thinking of her, though now, of course, I was thinking of her, which sent a dull ache to the center of my chest. Gulped from a new beer, then leaned forward and tried to breathe.

"It's worsest round about three o'clock in the morning," E.B. said. "That's when they commence to crank the shit wide open. They crank it up at night, see, when they think I'm sleeping."

Never noticed how often a person needed a deep breath until there came a pain in my chest that prevented one.

"That's when it's worsest. Round about three o'clock in the morning."

Twisted my mouth into a triangle, trying to inspire a pressure-relieving belch, but vomit rose instead, hovered, and fell back.

"I been smelling that shit since 1943, and I know for a fact it's got worse. Ain't a man alive smelled as much of that shit as I have. I been smelling it since 1943, when the white folks down to the shipyard was kind enough to let me and some other black folks work the graveyard shift when they weren't no white folks around. I been smelling that shit ever since then, in 1943."

Dropped an empty beer and popped a new one.

"You know they renamed our road after Dr. King, right. All the way up to your newspaper, I mean. You know why it stop there and become Newcastle? Because your publisher, Big Dick Taylor, he said he'd move the whole damn place over to St. Simons if he had to have that nigger's name on top his letterhead. I ain't lying. I got my sources."

A neighbor's tree-chained dog barked at every passing car. He'd been barking for awhile, but I'd just now registered the sound.

"Big Dick Taylor was talking about it one day down to the Shipwreck Lounge where he go every morning for his first one of the day. My buddy, Ray McRae, he was in there—he my source. He ain't that bright, but he got a pair of ears works alright. Big Dick said to the bartender, he said he wouldn't mind having Dr. King as the name of the road that went by his place so long as the rest of it could be named James Earl Ray Avenue. That's the honest to goddamned truth. And this beer's hot as hell. Ain't you got a refrigerator?"

Got up, took two steps to my left and urinated on a dead magnolia. The tree-chained dog next door pointed his barking at me. He barked while lying down. I sat down again and grabbed a fresh beer, and told E.B. I didn't feel much like talking over the traffic and the dog and my screaming blood.

"What?" he said.

"Said I don't feel like talking."

"You don't feel like talking?"

Nodded, but he didn't see.

"I'm trying to educate your stupid ass. What you ought to do is interview *me*. That's what you ought to do. You ought to be writing up some of the stories I be telling you. That's what you ought to be doing. Who else you know been around long as I have?"

"I need some silence."

"You need some silence?"

"And some darkness."

"Some darkness?"

"And some silence."

E.B. turned his good eye to me, pulled the tab from his beer can, dropped it inside and rattled the can. Handed him another one.

"Things has changed," E.B. said.

"There's only assembly lines," I muttered.

"What?"

"The job of the assembly line I'm on is to publicize every other assembly line."

"You mumbling."

"Marx said the worker was an appendage of the machine."

"You find that refrigerator?"

"I need a new country and a different language. Maybe Russia."

"Maybe Russia."

"You spend a lifetime working, and by the time you retire, what remains is a rainy weekend spent in front of the television."

"You living rent-free, you got you a respectable job, and you got me for a neighbor. What kind of problems you got?"

Drained my beer and dropped it. Watched gray-black smoke spew from the stacks into the clouds and bleed back out again.

"Only thing wrong with you is laziness."

"You think we could be quiet for awhile?"

"I can be quiet for a *long* while." He turned his head away. "I used to know this nice boy called me Uncle E.B. Where he at? Dead and gone *I* believe. He done went to college and come back a angry man who wants to go to Russia and be deaf. You want quiet? I'll give you quiet. I'll introduce you to the quiet of the grave, boy."

The traffic washed by in waves, and the tree-chained dog barked at every car.

E.B. turned on his radio to the Braves pregame show. Too loud. The tree-chained dog barked at a group of kids who taunted it with sticks. E.B. turned his radio up over the barking dog and screaming kids. Closed my eyes.

Mother pulled into the driveway and blew her horn so violently that I dropped a full beer into the dirt. I'd seen her just briefly the night before, but we hadn't talked. She was in bed when I arrived, so I didn't bother her, and when she left in the morning my face faced the back of the couch, and she didn't bother me. We had tried to be so quiet that neither knew the other was there.

She'd gained considerable weight, and took more time now distributing it from leg to leg. She stopped three feet in front of me, staring at empty beer cans and one spilled beer making a puddle in the dirt. She wore a dirty one-piece white uniform that smelled of a freezer full of bleeding shrimp. She slumped with a kind of poor posture I'd never seen. Wrinkles and loose skin were caked around the base of her neck, and brown spots had popped up on her hands. Her eyes didn't look parallel anymore. One eyebrow was slightly higher than the other, and they were flecked with gray. Her mouth was hanging open, and I could see a bottom tooth. Realized then that she'd never once stopped worrying. Tried to smile.

E.B. said, "Afternoon Miss Marjorie," but she didn't answer him.

I said, "Hey Mom," but she didn't answer me. She just slumped and stared, open-mouthed.

"It's not going to be like this," she said. She stared at me longer than necessary, sending serious doubts as to my age and relative maturity. Then she walked between E.B. and me and went into the house.

"Guess you heard that," E.B. said. "Ain't gonna to be like this."

Traffic blared past in all four lanes, and the sun began to sink. The tree-chained dog barked while lying down. E.B. turned up his game, a scoreless first inning recorded for history. Then a furniture salesman said teamwork was the difference.

"Ain't gonna to be like this," E.B. said.

A tractor salesman said don't be plowed under by paying too much.

The sun unhooked itself from its apex, and the heat grew softer. Tractor-trailers drove in lines. Smoke spewed from the stacks into the clouds and bled back out again. Dogs answered each other from all directions. A car salesman said it wasn't his job to sell me a car. It was his job, he said, to help me make choices.

"Ain't gonna be like this," E.B. said.

The sun sank, and a soft breeze stirred. Closed my eyes and looked for ways to leave. Saw myself looking through a window of a greyhound bus, slipping into the smells and voices of the desperate lives around me. Saw myself sitting in the shelter of an interstate overpass, backpack full of beer, and a cardboard sign saying, "anywhere." Then I pictured myself sitting in the spot where I was sitting, beer in hand, and more at feet, exhausting a life by picturing ways to leave.

4

Walked with my head down through the lobby, moving quickly past the beautiful receptionist I'd noticed the day before, but was too scared to speak to, even after she'd smiled and said good morning with such sincerity that for a moment I'd been fooled. Noticed now, from the corner of my eye, that she had noticed me, and when I looked at her, she looked back with the same smile she'd used the previous day, and for another moment I thought that the morning might be good. Smiled while stepping faster so she'd have less time to study my deformity—caused by nerve damage suffered at the age of three—effecting partial paralysis to the left corner of my mouth so that a triangle formed every time I talked, though it grew more prominent anytime I dared a lips-parted smile. With a lips-closed smile—which is what I offered now in passing—my mouth simply slid to the right side of my face, and since she was seated on my left, I barely smiled at all. Should have waved. Spent the morning thinking that I should have waved.

Descended the basement stairs and slumped in my straight-back chair. Mark and Mary Kay laughed into their phones with commissioners and cops. The fluorescent lights buzzed above. Certain spots of the urine-colored wall bumped and dipped, which gave it the texture of a newspaper soaked by morning rain and dried by afternoon sun. The buzzing lights birthed a headache so severe I had to close my eyes. Black clouds collided behind my eyes, competing for a view.

Opened a new document on my computer and stared at the blank screen, thinking of resignation.

Mary Kay said, "The apprehending officer recovered a refrigerator valued at $250 in the 700 block of MLK Jr. Blvd. at 23:50." She cradled her phone somewhere between her shoulder and chin and typed what she was hearing. She typed and then read back what she typed, going slow and easy for the sake of truth and accuracy. A profound sense of the dramatic entered her inflection, fear and trembling at the ugliness of crime.

She personalized every incident.

Mark said, "I know what you're saying, Buck. I have it word for word: privatizing waste management saves taxes. I know."

Two tons (I'd read) is the weight of the average cumulus cloud.

Big Dick Taylor said to Orville, "Is Toronto in Ohio?"

Mark said, "Yes, Buck—privatizing waste management is simply more practical. Plus, it would keep those bastards from ever striking again. Let's put that in there."

Four tons is the weight, on average, of a cumulus cloud collision.

Mary Kay said, "The apprehending officer recovered a window unit air conditioner, valued at $300, in the 1300 block of MLK Jr. Blvd." And then: "Oh my goodness."

Spent an hour writing a new first sentence to my resignation letter.

"Dear editor:

I've forgotten what I wanted to say, but it doesn't matter. What I've realized because of my forgetting is more important. What I've realized is that America's amnesia is caused by the noise inside of newsrooms.

Then deleted it.

After deadline, Little Dick walked toward me with a poster and taped the poster to the end of my desk. He said, "Congratulations," smiled with lots of teeth, and then returned to his desk. I rolled my chair around to look at the poster: "Business and Religion." He'd constructed the sign with red and black magic marker, uneven letters with lines slanting at ridiculous sloping angles like a kindergartener's finger-painting project.

In the coming days, it was clear that this would be my only job. Church secretaries from four counties bombarded me, delivering 2,000 year- old-news. They called me sugar and honey and invited me to church. They gave me pamphlets for my own use, and single Bible verses typed on laminated cards called "Strength for Daily Living," and Internet addresses for further learning, such as God.com.

Adel McDonald, of New Hope Pentecostal Temple of Revival for the Church of God that Christ Established, gave me three handwritten pages three times a week. She sat in the metal chair beside my desk and read them out loud to me so I could make suggestions. She raised her voice above the other voices in the room and recited her briefs as if reading from a picture book, pausing between paragraphs. Typical among them, this:

> Our pastor, the Rev. Calvin McDonald will preach this Sunday from Ephesians 6:10-18. His subject will be, "The Armor that Cannot be Penetrated." Sunday night, his text will be taken from Romans 8:35-39. We welcome visitors.
>
> Church members honored deacon Joel Blevins and his wife Susie with a surprise supper Saturday night on their 25th wedding anniversary. They received several nice and useful gifts.
>
> My husband and I visited my brother and his wife, Kevin and Ora Lee Hooper in Waycross Friday night. Kevin is home from the hospital after having his gall bladder removed. Prayers are appreciated.
>
> Get-well wishes and prayers go to our mailman, Tony Sales, whom came home Friday from the hospital after heart surgery. Everyone pray for Roberta Montgomery, who is going to the Miss Georgia Pageant. She is the daughter of Frank and Shelley Montgomery, and is a long-time member of the church handbells team. Happy birthday to Brenda Kicklighter on August 6th and to Susie Blankenship on Aug 8th.
>
> A household shower was given for Courtney Lyon and Mitch Wood Sunday afternoon in the church fellowship hall. They received several nice and useful gifts.
>
> At the Milton Library last Thursday morning at the summer reading program, Latreca Parsons had twelve children and twenty-three adults for her program on "Caterpillars." She read the book and gave a puppet show, "The Crazy Mixed up Caterpillar." Next Saturday, there will be a pet show. All the children will bring their pet.

Slumped in my chair as these women came to me. They were all perfectly nice, too perfectly nice, (like most people, I'd noticed now) and so I quickly agreed to whatever they wanted so I could get rid of them more quickly. Nodded often, but rarely looked them in their pastry-textured faces. Natalie Coleman brought leftovers from bake sales and chicken dinners. She put food on my desk and tried to negotiate the location of her articles.

"Couldn't you put mine up top?" she'd say. "With big bold letters?"

"Sure," I said.

"Like on the front page. Like those headlines have. You know, big and bold."

"Be glad to," I told her.

She said, "What's your favorite dessert, honey?"

"I like those Rice Krispie Squares you bring sometimes."

"I scratch your back and you scratch mine," she said. And then she'd laugh the laugh of all the church ladies who laughed because they knew the schedule for redemption.

Natalie's Briefs advertised church activities, typical among them this:

> The Potter's Wheel Pentecostal Holiness House of God in Christ Inc. will hold a youth day at 11:30 a.m. Sunday. The speaker will be William T. Cahoon, who will speak to the children on the Second Commandment. The event will include pony rides, a space walk, and the Cone County Fire department will talk to children about fire prevention. Also on hand will be the traveling evangelical ministry, "Cowboys for Christ," along with their horses. Lunch, including hot dogs, will be available for a small donation. There will also be special singing.
>
> Sunday night in the prayer room, 30 minutes before church services, Eve Moore will lead the first of fourteen study sessions on "Exploring the Fruit of the Spirit." This is a detailed look at the nine character traits that make up the fruit of the spirit—love, joy, peace, patients, kindness, goodness, faithfulness, gentleness, and self control.
>
> We have also began a new ladies Bible study and prayer time Friday's from 10 a.m. to noon with a women's day out scheduled for the fourth Friday in each month. This day out activity will alternate from mornings to evenings to accommodate women who work inside and outside the homes. Ya'll come!

Saw the same face every time a new face brought a business brief: the arrogance in the center of their eyes that advertised the high risks they could afford to stake, and the fear in the corner of their eyes that their high-risk news had to be trusted to someone like myself, who never once returned their enthusiasm—that most precious of commodities businesspeople can't understand the absence of, even in the faces of those who serve fast food. They smiled anyway, and laughed the laugh of hunters who need to charm you with a story.

They were orthodox members in the theology of pep.

Learned to tell time by the sound of Lisa Hedrick's heels clapping across the floor, and by her rattling bracelets, and by her perfume. She brought briefs announcing promotions and acts of humanitarianism from officers at First Georgia Coastal Bank. Brought me headshots of devout do-gooders and shots of suited men in hardhats whose shiny wingtips stood poised on the blades of shovels. Once a week she asked, while still smiling, why it was that her stories were relegated to the business section rather than the news section, and then she'd cock her head in a way that charged me with discrimination.

"I don't make the rules," I'd say.

"You're just following the chain of command," she'd say.

"That's right," I'd say.

"I can appreciate that," she'd say. And then she'd straighten her head and smile again, and ask whether that day's brief would make that night's paper.

And I'd say, "Yep."

Then she'd ask if I had questions concerning details of that day's briefs.

And I'd say, "Nope."

She'd ask if I had any follow-up questions about any other piece of news or activity being spearheaded by First Georgia Coastal Bank.

And I'd say, "Nope."

Then she'd smile and lift her shoulders and say, "I'll see you tomorrow then."

And I'd wave, rather than speak or smile, and grind my teeth while her clapping heels and jangling jewelry and stinking perfume traveled back across the newsroom.

In the pauses between brief-bringers I picked up my pencil and swept broad-brush strokes across my desktop calendar. Pressed hard to darken the lines around the edges. Licked my finger and smeared it across the center so the dark lines would bleed into the lighter lines. Slashed the page with strokes designed like horizontal rain. Tilted my pencil at forty-five degrees and smeared thick lead until the page disappeared, thinking myself talented in some odd and useless way. I obliterated August, the month of failed resignation. Then flipped the page and went to work on blank September.

5

On a morning toward the end of September, found mother still in bed. Her face was facing mine, and her breath was coming out as if a cracked whistle were lodged inside her lungs. The lamp on her bedside table was on, and a romance novel and her glasses lay on the bed beside her. Stared at her, wondering what to do. Felt creepy, staring so long, so I moved my eyes around the walls at pages torn and hung from *National Geographic*: one of the snow-capped Rockies, one of a geyser blowing steam in Yellowstone, one of a giant Redwood in California. She'd said she wanted to go out west and take in these things before she got too old. Neither one of us had ever been west of Atlanta, three hundred miles away, though we'd never been to Atlanta either. Throughout my youth, Atlanta was spoken of in proximity to the moon. Stood beside her bed and looked at the pictures on her walls, hoping her eyes would be open by the time I looked back at her. Thought to wake her, and then thought to let her sleep, then thought to wake her and ask if she needed anything before leaving her to sleep again. Planted my hands in my pockets and bent toward her.

"Mom," I said, not loud enough. Moved my hand toward her shoulder and drew it back without touching her. There was a person standing *inside* the Redwood tree, in an opening in the trunk, arms spread to show how the hands couldn't reach either side. Then mother's eyes cracked open, and this scared me so much, I let out an ineffectual little gasp.

"What's wrong?" she said.

"I was just seeing if you—"

"You're mumbling."

"If you were okay."

"I'm not okay."

"What's wrong?"

"I'm tired."

She closed her eyes and I looked at the walls. Her walls needed painting.

The whole house needed painting. Spider webs needed knocking down, the gutters needed emptying, mousetraps needed setting, the light bulbs in the hall and kitchen needed changing, the hinge on the screen door needed replacing, water spigots needed tightening, termites needed killing, and noises in the attic needed investigating.

"You need me to—"

"Why you whispering?"

"Do you need me to do anything?"

"No."

"Need me to—"

"What?"

"Do you need anything?"

"I need to rest."

"You need some juice?"

"I need to rest."

She closed her eyes and I looked at walls.

"I guess I'll go to work then," I said.

"Good."

"If you need to call."

"I need to rest."

She kept her eyes closed while she waved two fingers. I moved her glasses and her book to her bedstand and turned off her lamp. Then I walked down the dark hall on tiptoes, trying to be quieter than I had ever been in childhood so she wouldn't be disturbed.

She was still in bed that night. And again the next morning. And the following night. She'd been fired from the seafood plant for missing too many days without a doctor's note. She stayed beneath her covers, hair matted on one side from sleeping. In the evenings, I came in and stared down at her for a while without speaking. Then I'd clear my throat and offer something insignificant.

"Brought you a paper," I'd say.

She'd whisper thanks; say she'd get to it later. Then she'd cough and close her eyes and tell me she was getting better.

"I'm having awful dreams," she said.

Kneeled on the floor beside her bed to hear her better.

"*Awful* dreams," she said.

Waited for her to continue at her own pace, not wanting to make her tired.

"Dreamed my body was covered in leeches and you were just standing there trying to say something, but you couldn't. Your mouth was moving, but no words were coming out. You were just standing there staring. And then I dreamed I was in the hospital and I asked the nurse for a Coke, and she said all we have is Pepsi. Guess we should sell my car. Is your truck fixed?"

Told her it was. I'd spent my first paychecks buying rebuilt parts.

"Let's sell my car," she said. "The rent and the light bill's due. Soon as I get better, we'll find another car, though you might need to give me a ride for a little while. You'd do that wouldn't you? Would you give your mother a ride?"

"Yes ma'am," I said. "I'd give you a ride."

"We'll make it," she said. "Haven't we always made it?"

Knelt beside her, nodding, even though her eyes were closed.

"Don't worry about the phone bill," she said. "It never rings. And we can do without the cable, unless you especially need it. Do you need the cable, honey?"

Looked at her closed eyes, saying nothing.

"We'll make it," she said. "I might need your help for a little while—till I can get on my feet again. I'm sorry, honey."

"We'll make it," I said.

"I can't get warm. Bring me a blanket from the hall closet."

Brought her a blanket and spread it over her.

"We'll make it," she said.

Tiptoed backwards from her room. Went to the kitchen table and stacked empty beer cans next to bills, trying to account for the money I'd made, and why I now only had four dollars crumpled amidst loose change in my front jeans pocket. Cashed my paychecks ($306.21 net) at a liquor store which charged two dollars per every hundred for the service, and then gave them an extra fifteen dollars for a case of weekend beer to save the time of going to the cheaper supermarket. Gave $269.73 to a kid with a northern accent who managed a brightly painted auto-repair franchise, and who had patched my truck with short-life parts. Then went to Wal-Mart, looking for a toothbrush, and bought a $250 set of golf clubs. Shuffled absently down mile-long aisles, crossing and criss-crossing into other aisles, going with the traffic, searching for hygiene. Passed through a supermarket and a McDonald's, past chainsaws and gymnasiums for the home: weight benches and exercise bikes, basketball goals, tennis rackets and an entire aisle dedicated to golf. Remembered reading inside my tollbooth something about the healing power of exercise—how the act of sweating released the toxins that collected in the cavities of the mind and clouded thinking.

Took my clubs the next day to a driving range and humiliated myself among a line of guys who sent balls flying high and deep and true while I labored over worm-burners, low-hooks and slices, and all out whiffs. My clubs didn't sound like their clubs when balls were struck. They had titanium heads on graphite shafts and when they made impact it sounded like silver dollars dropping from the sky into pools of change. Woke the next morning with a sore stomach and never went back again. Kept the clubs in the back of my truck and, except when I rounded corners too quickly, forgot about them.

Gained fifteen pounds inside a month. My steps slowed, and my breathing grew more labored. My back gave way to constant cramping from sleeping on mother's loveseat, the place where I collapsed at the end of days and didn't move again, except to bring handfuls of drive-through food and beer from chest to mouth.

Drank beer and watched television, fighting sleep, because to give in to sleep would mean that the day had won. Gave in to sleep and drifted into dreams of fighting. Woke up tired, back twisted into knots. Woke at three and four a.m. and couldn't sleep again. I'd stare down the dark hall to the lamp coming from mother's room, and I wouldn't rise to turn it off. Stared down the hall and tried to calculate what percentage of a life is lost to working a job whose only value is to live with lights. Insomnia forced a focus to these late nights, and I sometimes stumbled upon a fragment I thought I could use in a resignation letter. Then I'd forget the fragment as soon as I was up and moving beneath the sun and among the voices. Went to work in wrinkled clothes and dirty shoes, belts wrapped around missed loops. Drove through dark and dreary mornings, houses and parked cars hazy with distortion. Sometimes the heads of other drivers resembled the shapes of long-nosed hogs.

6

Every second and fourth Monday night at 6:55 p.m., I rose from the couch, dead-eyed, in wrinkled clothes and matted hair, and drug myself to the cafeteria of an elementary school, where I filled a tiny orange chair at a table where there was taped a piece of notebook paper reading "PRESS." The room smelled of fish sticks and pizza squares. Eight school board members, the superintendent, and his lawyer sat behind tables placed in front of me, and passed a Mr. microphone—voices squawking from a boom box pointed just at me. Behind me, the same few people filled the same chairs every week: obese administrators who slouched and slept, and usually just one citizen, Chester B. Montgomery, who alternated between applause and protest.

In late August, Item IX of the agenda addressed the death of Dotty Kirkland, a second grader who had drowned in the pond behind the elementary school after her class had gone to observe some algae. She'd ventured away on her own to a distant corner of the pond and was left behind. Theorists believed she was trying to join a family of ducks, got in over her head and panicked.

Buck Jones, Superintendent, took a moment to express the grief the board felt over the tragic incident. He said the teacher who had failed to account for Dotty Kirkland had been dismissed and would never again teach in Georgia.

His recommendation was to drain the pond and fill it in with dirt, "In order to guard against any other such future tragedies which may or may not occur." *Robert's Rules of Order* prevented him, as Superintendent, however, from making such a motion, though if another board member saw fit to advance the motion, a vote could be taken. Cecil Goodbread then advanced the motion, which was seconded by Rev. Baker and approved unanimously with the sound of aye.

John Hampton then asked if there was any further business. Chester B.

Montgomery stood in the middle of the room and asked the board what they planned to do with all the fish, and if they had no objection, maybe he should go ahead and catch them all. An obese administrator then shifted in his seat behind me and asked why Chester alone should be entitled to all the fish. John Hampton banged his gavel. Cecil Goodbread said since the fish resided in a pond located on school grounds the fish were considered private property and anyone caught poaching would be subject to criminal charges of trespassing. Chester B. Montgomery yelled that Cecil just wanted the fish for himself. Goodbread denied the charge. "I've already *got* a freezer full of fish," he said.

John Hampton banged his gavel and asked for order. He said the issue currently in front of the board seemed to be the question of how to dispose equitably of the fish.

"Fry them," Rev. Baker said. "Let's hold a fish-fry and use it as a revenue generator toward the purchase of new band uniforms."

Alice Davenport said, "What about some flowers and trees for beautifying the grounds."

"How 'bout some tackling dummies," Harold Powell said.

John Hampton said *Robert's Rules of Order* specified the need to vote on one motion before proceeding to the next. He then recommended that the board table the issue of how to allocate the revenue until they knew exactly how much revenue the fish fry raised, if in fact the fish fry was something someone was going to make a motion toward.

In the form of a motion then, Rev. Baker proposed a fish-fry. Goodbread seconded the motion and it was approved unanimously with the sound of aye. Buck Jones suggested the second Saturday in December, when a celebration of sorts could be conducted for yet another year's worth of hard work, complete with annual awards given to recognize the truly dedicated.

"And with that," John Hampton said, "we stand adjourned."

After that meeting, my focus slipped. Couldn't pay attention. Grew hypnotized by the heavy breathing of narcoleptic administrators. Listened to the air conditioner clicking on and off. Zeroed in on the facial tics of Chester B. Montgomery. Compared the size and shape of moles on the necks and faces of the heads who wanted to save the children. Discovered resemblances in their heads and the heads of rodents. All the voices melted into mumbling that lulled my mind to sleep, even as my hand continued taking notes.

The next morning, under deadline, I wrote the stories based on the notes my hand had taken the night before. One Tuesday in October, I sat in the lawn chair facing Hank Snow, hands cupped around my mouth. He shook his head at me, even while he was staring at his desk. He seemed to have bad news. Looked over his head to the poster of the bald eagle. The eagle's pink eyes were cast in sorrow, and I knew why. The eagle needed corrective vision. Nearsighted eagles can't find fish, and their increased efforts lead to headaches. This eagle had a headache. Hank Snow looked up from his desk, and frowned at me, bad news coming.

"Buck Jones called," he said, "to say the cost of the new band uniforms the board approved is not $90,000 as you wrote—it's $9,000—to be deferred over the next three years. He said you also failed to mention that the last time they bought band uniforms was some nine years ago. You also failed to mention, he said, that the board passed around a current band uniform which clearly displayed a very worn and tattered condition—all of which means you get to write a correction which makes mention of these things. Is there any particular reason you're trying to get us sued?"

Kept my hands folded across my mouth, and stared at Hank Snow's ungroomed eyebrows, thick and unwieldy like Woodsy, the cartoon owl. Remembered then that board members had poked their fingers through the armpit holes of some garment, gasping and shaking heads, panicked over faded colors and the high school's image.

"What can I do?" Hank Snow said. "If there's something I can do to help you get better at this, Gray, I wish you'd tell me what it was." He leaned over his desk, eyebrows bunched. "I'll tell you a secret," he said. "No one's ever been fired from this newspaper. It's not that hard of a job. Listen, take notes, transcribe the notes into a basic inverted pyramid formula, going from most important to least important. I don't know, Gray. What do you have to say?"

Long gray hairs were scattered in his eyebrow patch.

"Well?" Hank Snow said.

One gray hair had separated from the rest and hung vertically in front of his right eye.

"Say something."

Wondered how he could see anything with that eyebrow in his way.

"Speak."

Spoke.

"What?"

Spoke again.

"Move your hands from in front of your mouth," he said.

"I've not been feeling ... my head." Pointed to my ear. "I think it's allergies." I'd never had allergies, but I'd heard people complain passionately about them, so I thought it appropriate to appropriate their pain. It bothered me that I couldn't think of anyone else in the world who shared a chronic failure to focus; someone I could reference for the sake of comparison. There was surely someone somewhere, but I imagined her in an institution, probably without a mother who had a loveseat for her to sleep on. Or she was in the streets of a larger city, where the odds were better for collecting change. Or she was locked comfortably inside a sound-proof room, secure in the belief that information is not knowledge and truth cannot be quoted. Looked above Hank Snow's head to the pink eyes of the nearsighted eagle and thought I was in the right mindset to write a resignation letter, but then I left the eagle's eyes and looked at Hank Snow, who seemed to be waiting for an answer to a question I had not heard.

"Well?" he said.

"Information is not knowledge," I said into my hands.

"Come again."

The truth cannot be quoted, I didn't say.

"Listen," Hank Snow said. "We all feel bad from time to time, but we have to be like football players, you know, we have to play hurt sometimes for the sake of the team. We have to reach down and see what we're made of."

Looked at his long gray eyebrow. "I'll—"

"Why are you still here?"

Wrote corrections, calling back Buck Jones, rechecking band figures from the past eight years. Typed and read back to Buck what I typed, apologizing for making him repeat himself.

In the middle of November, my early morning notes revealed a story involving a board member's proposal to install machine guns on every school bus.

Hank Snow called me to his office late that afternoon.

"Buck Jones called," he said. "Never at any time, he said, was there ever any mention whatsoever of machine guns. He went back and listened to the tapes of the meeting and never once heard machine guns mentioned. He has no idea where you might have dreamed that up. I'm sort of curious myself."

The eagle's nearsightedness was killing him. He was starving.

"Did any of your teachers growing up—did any of them ever think you might have some kind of a—what do you call it—some kind of a learning handicap—something like, what's it called—"

"Attention deficit disorder, or ADD, for which Ritalin is prescribed?"

"Yeah. Is that what you got?"

"No."

"Every time I walk through the newsroom I see you staring into space."

Couldn't remember Hank Snow ever walking through the newsroom, catching me staring into space, but I couldn't deny it was a good possibility.

"Some people, Gray, simply have to try a little harder than others."

"I realize—"

"Just get out there and concentrate."

"I'll make a—"

"Ask for help. I'll help. Mark and Mary Kay—they'll help. Starting tomorrow, I'd like to see a story a day from you. Talk to people on your beat. Talk to people on the street. Look around at what's going on. Just pay attention, Gray."

"It's just that—"

"Let me give you something to read." He opened a top desk drawer and pulled out a neatly folded article. "This is a story I wrote last year that won third place in a statewide contest. It took three minutes to write. You know why? Because I've been doing this for forty years. Everybody has to learn from somebody. Maybe you can learn something from it." He handed it to me and smiled.

Went to my desk and read his article, framed by two pictures Lester had taken—a close-up of a white-haired man stooping beside a rain gauge, and a picture of an open calendar marked with daily amounts of rainfall.

The Rain Marker
Milton retiree enjoys keeping daily account of the weather
by: Hank R. Snow, Managing Editor

Eight year-old Carlton D. Erwin bought his rain gauge at a yard sale seven years ago.

The owner wanted $1.50 but Erwin got it for a dollar.

In and around Milton, folks call him "the weather man."

At the Milton Senior Citizens Center, at McGill's Hardware Store, at Brian's Barbershop—people who know him know that he knows the weather.

"He keeps exact track of it," says Brian Carter, who has cut Erwin's hair for thirty years. "I can ask him, and he'll tell me exactly the dates of when it rained and how much."

But it wasn't always so.

Erwin grew up on an eight-acre farm outside of Nahunta, where he lived through most of his 20's. "I didn't pay it no attention then," he says.

Even so, a connection with the elements was already taking root. He recalls his dad telling him about the "rain crow," a small, brown dove that cries mournfully when it gets parched.

"When they holler for rain, most of the time you'll get it," he says.

His uncle taught him about the connection between moisture and the moon, advising him to slaughter hogs during full moons, when they're likely to yield the most lard.

"Most of the rest," Erwin says, "I picked up myself."

His wife, Wezee, supports his hobby. She gives him new calendars at Christmas in which to record daily rainfall measurements as well as high and low temperatures.

Flipping through his seven calendars, he notes a few memorable days.

"On Sunday, October 10, 1999, it rained all day and all night, and we got 12 inches. That adds up when you get it like that. But I'm just giving you the highlights. It doesn't always rain like that."

Even more striking was a rain that started August 26, 1995, the result of a tropical storm. Erwin recalls dumping four inches from his gauge before going to bed. Before church the next morning, he dumped six inches. He dumped six more when he returned from church and then six more Sunday evening.

"They's some people who don't believe that," he says. "But I can't help it if they don't believe it or not. I'm not competing with nobody; I just put down what it was."

Erwin enjoys weather-watching, but he's cultivated other hobbies too, especially because of a nerve disorder called neuropathy, which keeps him inside more than he would like.

He likes recording old movies and TV shows—he has about 200 episodes of *The Lone Ranger*, and is now collecting Andy Griffith episodes on DVD.

But he's best known for keeping track of the rain.

"It's just interesting," he says. "It's something I like to do. They call me the weather man."

7

Scanned the AP wire one dull morning in November and discovered my cursor was alive inside the text, which meant I was free to edit stories before they went to World Briefs in section C. Read of a stampeding herd of elephants destroying villages in India, and for every mention of a village, I substituted the names of small towns in Southern Georgia, so that forty people were crushed to death in Hoboken, and a hundred huts were squashed in Hortense. There were stories of earthquakes and flooding and general pestilence in remote corners of the world, and I localized every incident, so that five hundred people in Vidalia were reported dead from famine and a thousand people in Jeff Davis County were dead from Malaria. Moved a cyclone from Bangladesh to Baxley, where it killed a thousand salt workers making $3.15 a month. Moved wars from Albania to Albany, where four hundred died from shelling. A frog with four heads was found in Thalman, a strain of E-Coli bacteria was sweeping over Sea Island, and a swarm of locusts had devoured a thousand acres of peanuts in Plains, including the plantation owned by Jimmy Carter.

Read the paper that night to see how much of my work had gotten through, and was surprised to see that elephants had indeed trampled huts in Hortense; that flood waters were roof level in Waycross. I localized catastrophes for a week, and waited for Hank Snow to call a meeting, but nothing was ever said. Waited for the calls of confused readers who would want to know if the flooding and disease were growing nearer. But no one noticed. No calls came, except for one. Chester Montgomery called to say that it was Time.

"Tell them the hour is here," he said.

"Yes," I said.

"It's your job, Leo," he said. "Your calling. To spread the word."

"Yes."

"The righteous are those who spread the word, Leo Gray."

"I'm spreading it," I said.

"Let's have us a meeting on God's golden shore."

Wondered who would take the minutes.

Then Chester hung up, and I survived the day because my work had finally reached someone.

8

Took mother juice and soup with buttered saltines on a tray. She fluttered her hand toward the bed stand, saying she'd get it later. The hair on one side of her head was flat, and pillowcase creases ran perpendicular to the wrinkles on her face. She closed her eyes and started talking. She talked softly and I had to kneel on the floor so my ear would be closer to her mouth.

"I had another awful dream," she said. "I went to step on a roach and it turned into a rat. Are there any rats in the kitchen?"

"I don't think so. I haven't seen any rats, Mother."

"I had another one. It was my birthday, and you gave me a box of shrimp with scorpions mixed in. Now why would you have done something such as that?"

"I wouldn't do that, Mother."

"Why would you give your mama a box of shrimp with scorpions mixed in?" She opened her eyes and stared at me, unblinking.

"I would never do that, Mama."

She sighed heavily, closed her eyes and whispered that she was getting better.

"Is there anything I can do for you?" I said.

"What?"

"Do you need anything?"

"A little thing of peanut butter. That works about the best of anything. But don't get any expensive kind. They can eat cheap. You ought to set a couple traps in E.B.'s place too. I bet that's where they're coming from."

"Yes, Mother."

"You got enough money for a couple of mousetraps?"

Told her yes.

"Go on then and get some. Their babies will be having babies by the time you get back."

Stood and stared at her and paused. Her eyes were closed and she was saying something I couldn't understand. Leaned closer, asking her to repeat herself, and she whispered again that she was getting better.

"We'll all be better soon," she said.

"Yes, Mother."

"Except I can't get warm."

Took her the blanket from my loveseat and spread it over the last blanket I'd gotten from the closet.

"Thank you, Leo."

"Your welcome, Mother."

She closed her eyes and I walked softly out of her room and returned to the porch to drink with E.B., who I had to nudge awake. Black smoke spewed from the smokestacks into the clouds and bled back out again. The trees dripped wetness and passing cars slashed puddles. The whole world was wet, but I couldn't remember it having rained. Couldn't remember a day when the sky was a different color and I couldn't imagine any day in the future when it would be less dreary.

Put a beer in the old man's hand and listened to him start a story.

"You know," he said, "I was throwing trash up in Albany in 1962 when the shit hit the fan there. Saw Reverend King get arrested. I was with all those people when they marched into that courthouse and stood in front of that sheriff there. I got the hell out of there and came back here, went to work at B&W 'fore they shut down—drank out a hot garden hose while white folks drank ice water in the shade. Late as 1972, black folks was still drinking from that garden hose. Where's that story? You better be writing this shit down."

When an old person dies, it's like a library gets burned, Alex Haley said, I read. So I drank beer and let E.B. talk, thinking I might remember something he said sometime when I needed it, but I already knew that all I would remember would be the feeling of regret for knowing I would not remember.

9

Hank Snow told me this: "Two things you don't fuck up in the newspaper business, Gray: wedding announcements and obituaries. Fuck them up, families hold a lifelong grudge, ruin our credibility by word of mouth, and cancel their subscriptions, which would cost us $156.00 in annual revenues per family if you figure fifty cents a day for six days a week, as we don't publish on Sundays, as you know."

The proper protocol was to follow the format of Jane Doe. I placed Jane's obit next to the obit of Beulah Lillian Blankenship, 64, of Milton, and tried to focus.

Mark and Mary Kay manufactured noise.

Mark said, "I know what you're saying, Buck. Waste management is expensive."

Mary Kay said, "How do you spell that officer's name?"

Jane Doe's obit said don't give a name to the cause of death. Readers needn't be disturbed. The word *death* itself is enough to bear. Write only the day and place. *Ms. Blankenship died Tuesday at her home.* I filled in the rest. *She died in her favorite living room chair, legs covered in the afghan her mother knitted in the same chair. It was the house Beulah had grown up in, the house she left at twenty after being married in the back yard, and the house she came back to at thirty-five, after her divorce. Beulah's mother then slowly died from cancer—skin peeling from her back as Beulah bathed her—and Beulah cared for her in the evenings, bringing her food on a TV tray. They watched murder mysteries and reenactments of real life crime. Beulah kept it her mother's house after her mother died—winding all the same clocks that had secretly gotten on her nerves; watering all the flowers she had thought a nuisance. She spent her nights alone, staring at the locks on doors. She died, finally, of nervousness—or more precisely, from the strain of trying so hard to keep her nervousness concealed. Beulah was sixty-four, a year before retirement, and therefore never owned her life. She was a year away from a full-time pursuit of whatever passion had been robbed from her while she exhausted herself working a job she hated so she could keep the house and buy herself groceries on double coupon day, treating herself on Sundays to a prime rib roast. Or either she was a year from growing unbearably still and lonesome, suddenly away from all the people who had witnessed her efficient and reliable production from her desk, and her pleasant nerve-hiding smile during cigarette breaks in stairwells. It was the accumulation of these simple exchanges during the course of the day that she replayed at night that made her feel less anonymous. She might have been a year away from killing herself. She spent her nights staring at her telephone.* On the line next to survivors, Jane Doe had a family listed—a husband, John, and two children—Jack and Jill. On the line next to survivors in Beulah Blankenship's obit there was a zero. *She was, like me, an only child, childless herself. A stranger to her neighbors, though they waved politely while backing out of driveways at eight a.m., and waved again pulling into them at five. Her life was lost to work, and there were no survivors. There are no survivors when your life is lost to work. When your life is work your life is lost. When your work is life your work is lost. Your life is lost.* Jane Doe allows a sentence to summarize a life: she worked fifty years for the *Coastal Georgia Sun*, was a member of First Baptist Church, and was an avid birder. *Beulah's life was like Jane Doe's, except that she worked at a different place and attended a different church, and apparently wasn't avid enough at anything for anyone to notice what she was avid at. She spent her nights staring at her hands. She stared at the black ink that leaked from the evening newspaper, which she read avidly each evening, obituaries and engagement announcements of people she wished she knew.*

Then I wrote my obituary/resignation letter:

My life expired Tuesday at my desk.

Surviving is the desk.

I was an avid lister of resentments, a devout believer only in step ten of the twelve steps trodden by the terminally recovering. I most avidly resented the busy champions of business and religion—thieves of time and stillness. I worked for them, producing noise.

Heard Hank Snow's footsteps and saw his short body from my periphery, so I deleted my new resignation letter, which also deleted Beulah's obituary, which meant by the time Hank Snow stood over my left shoulder, my computer screen was blank. It was ten a.m. Two hours of my life had been exhausted creating Beulah's obit, though there was nothing now to show for it.

Hank Snow leaned over my shoulder and whispered in my ear. "Deadline is upon you."

Stared at my blank computer screen, saying nothing.

"Jesus Christ, Gray," Hank Snow said. "You haven't even started that obit?"

"It vanished," I said. "Disappeared."

"Three minutes," Hank Snow said. He walked briskly back to his office, making a show of shaking his head.

The next morning, Hank Snow said I'd left out the paragraph in Beulah's obit which was supposed to list the preacher presiding over the funeral service, an omission brought to light late the night before, when the presiding preacher called Hank Snow at his home, threatening to cancel his subscription and ruin our credibility by word of mouth. I sat in the lawn chair facing Hank Snow, not knowing what to say.

"What do you have to say?" he said.

Said I didn't know.

He paused, cocked his head at an angle and tried a softer tone.

"What can I do to help, Gray? Whatever I can do to help you get better at this, I'll do. Just tell me what it is." He slumped in his leather chair, face already drained of answers.

"Not feeling," I said.

"Speak up."

"Said I'm not feeling."

"Not feeling well?"

"Not feeling."

"Why didn't you say so, Gray? Shit, I'm not some kind of a tyrant who's going to dock you for not feeling well. If the way you're feeling is adversely affecting our product, in fact, I would encourage you to go home. What if it were something more serious? What if, instead of simply omitting something, you had accidentally libeled someone and gotten us sued? What if it were something more serious such as that?"

"Just not feeling."

"Take the rest of the day off and come back tomorrow feeling rested."

Nodded.

"Feel better," Hank Snow said.

10

Went to Wal-Mart and bought for mother a $300 sixteen-inch television with a built-in VCR. Put it on the dresser at the foot of her bed, and handed her the remote. And then I went in at four and five a.m. to turn it off, trying not to look too long at her upturned sleeping face and the saliva streaming from one side of her cracked mouth. Stood there sometimes in the blue light of the television looking at her face, wondering whether I should remove her glasses. This would require, however, my needing to look too closely at her sleeping face, which would force me to see into the bottom of every wrinkle, and at the crossroads of certain wrinkles there lived stories I didn't want to hear. There were stories of a drunken father who drowned during the family's one excursion to the beach. There were stories of a mother now dying in a home with demented memories appropriating the pasts of aristocrats. There were wrinkles telling stories of sisters who moved out west, changed their names and became invisible. There were wrinkles that talked of a long-gone husband who never talked or touched, who lived in the tradition of southern men who surrender their aloofness with sentimental tears only at the death of cowboys. Then flee. There were wrinkles inspired by an only son who threw things in his youth, battering furniture and bruising walls, leaving finally after stealing money. There were wrinkles beneath wrinkles which spoke of work: wrinkles carved while standing for twelve hours in subfreezing rooms, plucking baby shrimp from a rattling conveyor to fill boxes shipped all over the world. Wrinkles formed from working sixty and seventy-hour weeks so she'd be tired enough at the end of the day to fall quickly into sleep, the only thing that kept her from having to think about her wrinkles.

So I left her glasses on, and tiptoed from her room as quietly as possible, holding my breath to make sure she wouldn't be disturbed.

She'd spent Thanksgiving in bed, and I'd spent it on the couch, watching football games I knew I would forget. The room was coated in shadow, and I napped, half-waking to voices of expert commentary. In one moment of wakefulness, I declared all holidays and weekends to be a waste—hours given for the recuperation from work so one could merely work again. Air pockets amidst a drowning. The plea bargain struck at the end of slavery.

The paper counted down days to Christmas, using a front-page box.

Bought mother $150 worth of amusing movies, and a $35 brass opera mask. Saw the smiling face on the outside of the box and thought if she hung it on her wall and stared at it long enough she might smile back at it. Had it wrapped in the mall, donating a dollar for a church, and then took it to her bedroom. She carefully tore the tape, meaning to save the paper. Pulled out a brass face of someone crying. I hadn't known there were opposing faces.

"How thoughtful," she said.

"They gave me the wrong one. I wanted the other one. There's one of a person smiling. That's the one I wanted. I'll take it back."

"I sort of like this one," she said. "I'll keep this one." She put the frowning face on her bedside table, propped against the lamp so it was facing her. She closed her eyes and said, "Thank you, Leo."

Stared at the wrinkles layered on the loose flesh of her neck.

She apologized, with eyes closed, for not being able to get me anything.

"I don't need anything," I said.

"We'll have us a good Christmas next year," she said.

"I know. It doesn't matter. You want me to put a movie in?"

"Okay."

Thumbed through the stack of movies, trying to find the right one. Picked one and put it in, and then ejected it, and put in another.

"Okay, Mama. It's starting."

"Okay, Leo."

Backed out of her room, reading the wrinkles on her eyelids.

Ate Christmas dinner with E.B. Miller, ham sandwiches with Duke's mayonnaise and Pabst Blue Ribbon beer. It was sixty-five degrees, and by universal definition, a bright and beautiful winter day.

New Years Eve, I spent with E.B. Miller, drinking beer, though we both went to bed before midnight, neither of us mentioning anything about the start of something new.

11

Ripped December from my desktop calendar, crumpled it and pounded it in my palms and against my desk. Squeezed it into the tiniest ball I could, reducing it until it could no longer be reduced, and then I slammed it in my metal wastebasket. The sound bounced against the near wall and traveled to the opposite wall above Orville Ledbetter's head and came back again, showcasing the bad acoustics of the room. Mary Kay watched in terror. Mark looked on with scorn. Felt sandwiched between their stares, but I didn't acknowledge them. Continued staring at balled-up December lying in the bottom of my wastebasket, and didn't acknowledge them at all.

"Do we feel better?" Mary Kay said. She held her phone daintily out beside her face, covering the mouthpiece to protect her cop's ear from the disturbance. When I wouldn't look at her, she went back to her cop, apologizing too sincerely. Mark picked up his phone, and turned his back to me, and a second later I heard Hank Snow's phone ringing in the distance. Mark complained in whispers to Hank Snow about the noise. Heard him whisper that his work was being compromised. Heard Orville Ledbetter chuckle softly across the room. Heard a matched-pitch sigh from Doris and Eula in *Coastal Life*. Heard them move their glasses to the ends of their noses. Heard them roll their eyes. Heard the overhead footsteps of a heavy lady in advertising returning from Krispy Kreme. Heard a maintenance man behind the urine-colored wall release a drop of oil onto the printing press.

Picked up my pencil and went to work on January. Turned my pencil on its side, and swept wide arcs across the center of the page. Darkened the lines at the top and bottom with broad brush strokes and left an opening in the center. Worked around the opening, darkening and erasing, licking my finger and smudging—until the opening resembled a sonogram of a deformed fetus. Thought I heard that thing that people claim to hear when they stumble upon a moment when they claim God is calling them. Heard Him tell me I was a doodler. Heard Him tell me to clean out my father's old shed in the back yard and convert it into a studio for doodling. Heard Him tell me to run extension cords and hang track lighting. He said to sit before my easel through the silence of the nights and doodle deep into the morning. I heard Him.

On my lunch hour, drove to a Christian bookstore located inside a pink mini-mall and bought $175.87 worth of art supplies. Bought eight different sized canvasses, an easel, three packs of acrylics, two dozen tubes of oils, a pallet, a smock apron, and sixteen camel hair brushes of different widths. Gathered these things and took them in separate trips to the counter. The big-haired lady behind the counter said, "Oh, an artist," and for the briefest moment, I believed her.

I knew nothing of painting, but I knew I needed to honor the craving. Decided the thing to do was abandon my resignation letter and paint a picture I could present to Hank Snow on my last day of work. But I knew nothing of painting. All I owned was an illusory confidence that I could combine colors and objects and come up with—what's the word artists use to describe the personality of light and shadow?

Sat at my desk through the afternoon, doodling over January, thinking of things I'd like to paint. Decided my paints would be—what was the word to describe the way certain artists captured the reality of distortion?

The newsroom was quiet. Mark and Mary Kay avidly tracked stories on their beats, and Little Dick Taylor worked doggedly to make a colored graph of yesterday's website opinion poll, where readers become actively engaged in shaping the discourse of their community by choosing one of two choices Little Dick gave them about spending $7.3 million to renourish beaches. Little Dick tabulated results, cussing to himself about the stupidity of people, and I doodled over January, looking for things to paint.

Focused on a single screw stuck in the center of the yellow wall. Beneath the screw was an outline of a rectangle where for many years there had hung a framed certificate. The yellow inside the rectangle was a sharper shade than the yellow around it. Wanted this empty space to be the subject of my first painting. Wanted to capture the contrast of yellow in the space around the empty space and I wanted to paint the screw that held the empty space in place.

Chiaroscuro was the word that meant what you got from the personality of light and shadow.

Doodled preliminary sketches over the month of February. Church ladies and business ombudsmen dropped off briefs and I stacked them in a corner, refusing to advance chitchat that would prolong their visits. Answered my telephone three times to make it stop ringing, and pretended to take messages.

Skewed was the word that described the realism of distortion.

When I got home, I didn't join E.B. on the porch and I didn't go inside to check on Mother. Carried my easel and my palette to the back yard and laid them in the grass beside my father's shed. Hadn't thought the shed would be so dilapidated. The tin roof, orange from rust, held holes the size of grapefruits, and every board had shrunk and shriveled. The shed door had separated from its hinges, but thick weeds and dirt had grown up in front of it and kept it sealed. Spread my arms and put a hand on each side of the door, lifted it, and threw it aside.

No room for a single step. The shed was a museum for the failed remnants of a life: washing machines, dryers, dishwashers, car hoods and fenders, skeletons of riding lawn mowers, stacks of rakes and shovels and posthole diggers, handsaws, hacksaws, and trays of loose nuts and bolts. Rotting lumber was stacked on top of rusted appliances—lumber saved for the day my father intended to build a new and better shed. Dense spider webs seemed to hold everything together. Only small patches of the dirt floor were visible. Inched forward, and scraped my left hand against a sharp wall of rust—the crumbling side of an ancient freezer. The back of my throat began to burn from dust— a burning that would remain except for the moments when beer later washed over it. Picked up my easel and palette and threw them inside the shed. Lifted the door from the yard and put it back in the groove between the dirt and weeds.

The next day, I traded my truck for a brand new sports car.

12

At the end of February, I stood in front of Eve, trying to say things I didn't know how to say. Moved the red half-moon magnet from the out slot to the in-slot and back again three times, and when she finally looked up from her magazine, I smiled.

"What's wrong?" she said.

Kate had worked with me on my smile. She'd said to lift both corners of the mouth at once, and to ensure symmetry, make sure the bottom lip touched the underside of my overbite. Show plenty of teeth, and spread a hint of the smile into the eyes. I practiced on inanimate objects. Pulled forks from drawers and showed them my pleased surprise. Snuck up on doorknobs, and greeted them like lost love. Watched Andy and Barney school Ernest T. Bass on how to make an entrance. Kate said teach the muscles and they'll remember.

But my muscles had forgotten. I stared, blank-faced, and thought of filling the pause with an honest account of my inability to smile. But I never knew what to say when I wanted to be sincere, so I didn't say anything at all. Moved my red half-moon magnet from the "in-slot" to the "out-slot," and back again. She looked me in the eyes without smiling, and then she turned and smiled to someone stepping loudly into the lobby. Lester dropped his camera bag at his feet and moved his half-moon magnet from out to in.

"You heard the news?" he said. He looked to me and then to Eve and back to me. He reeked of coffee and cigarettes. No one answered him, so he told us.

He clapped me on the shoulder and said, "looks like Clark Kent here is been promoted. You better follow me."

Descended the basement steps and walked across the newsroom into Hank Snow's office, which Little Dick now occupied, adorned in coat and tie, drawing blue lines against a ruler on a dummy page.

"Morning, boss," Lester said.

Little Dick didn't look up. He said, "You got a file photo we can run four columns—something with kids on the beach or something?" Then Little Dick turned to me and said, "Congratulations. You're our new Business and Religion Editor. You need to get the business page laid out for today. You know how to design and lay out a page, right? Didn't you go to journalism school?"

"No. What happened to Hank?"

"He took a job with the DNR to conduct a bird census. Layout isn't that tough. Just figure out how long your stories and briefs are and then measure out the same number of inches to fill the columns on the page, working around the ads, which have already been laid out, and then chop the briefs or articles if they're too long, or fill them, or space them if they're too short. Better get chopping."

"Better get chopping," Lester said. He threw his head back and disappeared, belly laugh bouncing down the hall.

Flipped the page and doodled over March.

Leonard hung up his phone and swiveled his chair to me, forearms resting on his thighs.

"Congratulations," he said. He stood up then, dropped a pencil on his desk and walked down the hall—gone before I could say that I hadn't asked for this—that I didn't want it, and that I'd soon be leaving, making vacant the position.

Lester approached my desk, camera hung around his neck.

"Need a headshot," he said. "Little Dick's going to run your picture on the back page."

"What for?"

"Don't ask me questions like that. Little Dick said take your picture, so that's what I'm doing. We need to go outside."

"What for?"

"My flash ain't working."

"Can this wait till after deadline."

"I'm *on* deadline, Clark."

Walked into Little Dick's office, and tried to register my discomfort of having my picture in the paper.

"It's news," Little Dick said. "The community needs to know we have a new Business and Religion editor."

"I'd really rather—I don't want—"

"I'm using it on the front page."

"You mean the back page?"

"Same thing. Hurry, so Lester can get it developed."

Lester propped me beside a palm tree, and made me squint into the sun, directing my posture while he focused.

"Lift your chin," he said. "Shoulders back. Chin up."

Gave him my fullest lips-parted smile, hoping the face that showed up in the paper might be skewed. But I never looked. I hadn't looked at the paper in several months. Once in a while I glimpsed a paper on someone else's desk and saw my byline, but it meant nothing. Every time I saw my byline, it looked like someone else's name.

13

Went to Mother's room at four a.m. to turn off her television. On the rare nights when her eyes were open, she motioned me to lean close so I could hear her nightmares. I knelt beside her bed and listened, saying nothing.

"I dreamed we were on a boat ride, except the boat was hooked to the back of a truck and we were being pulled down these long dirt roads. We were still having a good time though, looking out at the scenery into the woods, just like we were on a lake or something, except then all of a sudden I was lying in a sandbox in the back of the boat and you were covering me with sand. Then the bombs were falling, and I couldn't find you. People were running and screaming and everything was burning, and then I found you at the bowling alley. I screamed for you to come on, but you said you were throwing a perfect game and couldn't leave." She closed her eyes and said that was all she could remember.

Knelt beside her until I knew that she was sleeping, and then I turned off her television and walked quietly out of her room and down the hall.

Some nights, she woke up as soon as I turned off the television and asked me to leave things the way I found them. She wanted to hear the noise of the television, and to see its light. I'd apologize and leave quietly again.

She complained constantly of being cold. One night, between narratives of nightmares, she said: "It's like I can't get out of that cooler."

"What cooler, Mother?"

"Where they keep the shrimp."

Bought her an electric blanket and she complained that it raised our electricity bill.

"I'll be alright soon," she said. "Soon as summer gets here. I'll be alright then," she said. And she closed her eyes and fell into sleep again.

Some nights I didn't enter her room at all. I stayed on the couch and refused to check on her, because I didn't want to see her upturned face and the saliva that dripped from one corner of her open mouth while she twitched inside her nightmares. When I half-woke at four a.m., I sometimes stared at her light bleeding into the hall and couldn't move again, because I knew that she was dying and that I'd be alone, and it scared me too badly.

14

If I ordered the fries I'd be stuck with a decision on whether to cut them clumsily with my fork or fold them with my fingers into my mouth; acts made easier with limber fries than with well-fried fries, the latter of which was the kind of fry I predicted would be the product of this place, Southern Oaks Barbecue, and which is why, finally, I went with the baked potato. Eve had the fries.

She had made the date, of course. She'd commented on my new car again one morning and suggested it might be nice to take a ride, possibly over lunch. It was a warm day in mid-March, and there were signs in the near-dead foliage that made me think Spring was something I should have been looking forward to. It was our first lunch together, and I was nervous because I wanted to call it a date, though Eve showed no signs of calling it anything but lunch. She seemed indifferent. She refused to advance any innuendo. Southern Oaks Barbecue was her idea, because we could stay in the car and let the girl on roller-skates take care of everything. Eve reclined her head against the seat and read the billboards that surrounded the parking lot like a fence.

"You ever notice," she said, "how so many advertisers think the fastest way to your wallet is to amuse you?"

Looked at her neck and nodded. I knew I wouldn't be able to eat, because I was fixated now on her neck, which I wanted to lean over and lick.

She pointed to a billboard in front of us and read: "A-1 Septic Tank: number one in the number two business, where a good flush always beats a full house. There's even an advertisement for another restaurant—Gilbert's Seafood: It Ain't Been Long Since They Was Swimming."

Her perfume mixed with the new car smell and lit a match inside my loins.

"Look at this guy." She pointed to her far right to a billboard which held the head of Zachariah Nebulous Linney, and beside the head a balloon with cartoonish letters saying this: 'My job is not to sell you a car. My job is to help you make choices.'—Please," Eve said. "Would you buy a car from that clown?"

"No way."

"Is that where you got this?"

"What?"

"This car we're sitting in."

"Are you kidding?"

"It is, isn't it?"

"You wouldn't believe the deal I got."

She squinted one eye at me for a half-second, and I looked away, to my left, where inside a sporty new truck sat the fattest man I'd ever seen. He gripped a sandwich with both paws, taking one, two, three bites before he pulled it back again.

The girl on roller-skates rolled back with a red tray she hooked on our respective doors. She rolled away again, and I looked at her muscular legs in my rearview. All my failures with women throughout high school kept me perpetually interested in high school women. When I rolled down my window, I heard the fat man's radio, tuned too loudly to the expert commentary of another fat windbag.

"I have an idea," Eve said. "Let's trade deep dark secrets." She broke a fry in half and placed both halves into her mouth, working her full lips over them while she kept her eyes locked on mine.

"Dark secrets?"

"*Deep* dark secrets. Being utterly honest, like secure adults."

Dug my plastic fork into my potato, snapping off two middle prongs.

"I'll go first, if it'll be easier," she said. "I've aborted three babies fathered from three different men and never told any of them." She kept her eyes locked on my eyes, her stoic face a sheet of calm.

"That's a good one," I said.

She moved her lips over another fry, and I felt my stomach knotting.

"How'd your parents take it?"

"I didn't tell them either. I've had two daughters since then anyway, now ages eight and five, by yet two different men with whom I was fleetingly involved and who now have full custody—yet four more secrets, which, according to my tally puts me up by about seven secrets."

"That's impressive," I said. "I can't compete with that."

"It's not a competition, stupid. It's a quick way to develop trust and intimacy."

"It's just that I'm fairly innocent."

"You have a sixty second reflection period, starting now."

Watched the fat man unwrap the plastic from another sandwich. Shifted in my seat, and rolled up my baked potato. Wanted the subject to get around to love, and then possibly to sex, or to sex and then to love. Wanted both of them at once. Wanted to be a gentleman, and I wanted to be sophisticated about it, but I wanted both sex and love, or both love and sex, though I didn't know how to get to it.

"Time's up," she said.

"I wet the bed until sixth grade."

"That's not a secret."

"How'd you know?"

"I mean it's not altogether uncommon, nor is it especially deep or dark."

"I was kicked out of the Cub Scouts."

"Uninteresting."

"I was fleetingly engaged and then unmercifully dumped."

"Better."

"She's a speech pathologist, and she fell in love with one of her clients, a paraplegic in a wheelchair."

"Very good. Now take us back to work."

"She lives in Charlotte and she was supposed to join me here— it was her idea, in fact. To join me here. Said we'd make a life, raise children by the ocean."

"Interesting. But we need to go. I only get a half hour lunch."

"The only way I can get to sleep is to drink myself to the verge of passing out, which is not really sleeping, except that it keeps me from thinking very bad things about myself and my future health."

"The reason I only get a half-hour—"

"But I always wake up at four a.m. and can't get back to sleep again."

"Is because little Dick says things are tight and he needs all the advertising ladies out in the field instead of covering the switchboard for an hour."

"I lie still and listen to my mother breathing, and I think—"

"Even though he just paid $37,000 for a year's membership to his Island Club."

"I think—"

"And $80,000 for a custom Range Rover."

"I think—"

"And $300,000 for a goddamn condo."

"I think about whether I'm dead."

"It makes you wonder."

"Yes."

She looked at her watch. The fat man ate another sandwich.

"Can we please go, please," she said.

"I'm writing a resignation letter."

"Little Dick makes note of tardies."

"I work on it between assignments."

"Three tardies equals one reprimand."

"It has to be perfect."

"One reprimand equals being docked one hour's pay, even if you only take half-hour lunches."

"The truth is, though, I'm nowhere close to finishing."

"So far I have two tardies, though neither was my fault."

"The truth is—"

"Barbara, in advertising, has one reprimand."

"The truth is, I don't know where to start. But I think—"

"And if I'm tardy today, I'll be forced to tell him it was your fault."

"I think—"

"Though he won't believe me."

"I think my resignation letter is the only thing that makes me believe I'm alive."

"And I'll lose an hour's pay, which perhaps you could see fit to reimburse me."

She looked at her watch. The fat man ate another sandwich.

I said, "Can we have dinner?"

"I have plans."

"A boyfriend?"

"That's personal information."

"I have plans too."

"You're lying."

"Am not."

"Are too."

"I was willing to break them, but not now."

"Maybe we can have lunch again sometime," she said.

"I'll have to check my calendar."

"Can we go?"

"We're going."

The fat man wiped his mouth.

15

Three days later, I stopped doodling and picked up my ringing phone. It was Eve, calling from upstairs, wanting to know what I was doing for dinner. I answered honestly, that I would probably do what I normally did, which was pick up a hamburger from a drive-thru on the way home, getting something for my neighbor too, maybe super-sized.

"I'm having a small dinner party tonight at seven," she said. "Can you come?"

She named the address, on Sea Island, and I panicked. Imagined men in tailored suits and women in glittering dresses discussing stocks and bonds while plucking tooth-picked olives from silver trays. Imagined myself slumping in a dark corner, blending in with plants while getting potted on champagne.

"What time?" I said.

"I told you: seven. I'm house-sitting, though I can't tell you whose house it is."

Remembering what I'd heard of protocol, I asked what I could bring. Then I wondered if I was supposed to ask at all. I think I was supposed to simply show up with gift in hand, and let the hostess satisfy the protocol of appearing pleasantly surprised.

"A bottle of wine," Eve said, and I panicked again. Didn't know my wines the way a cultivated man was supposed to know his wines.

"Okay," Eve said. "I'll tell you whose house it is, but if you tell anyone, we'll never speak again."

"Maybe you'd better not tell me."

"It's Big Dick Taylor's. Our former CEO and publisher. He's in Palm Springs, and asked me to house-sit for him. He always liked me. See you at seven."

Spent an hour piecing together my evening outfit, donning the navy sports coat mother bought me in high school which still hung in my closet, never worn, and which was now a full size or two too small. The cuffs stopped short of my wrists, and I stood in front of the bathroom mirror and pulled them, thinking it might help. Stood in front of mother next, beside her bed. She said I looked nice, though my shoes badly needed shining. She closed her eyes and coughed and motioned me to come closer.

"Keep your napkin in your lap, and your elbows off the table."

"Yes, Mama."

"Stand up when a lady enters the room."

"Okay, Mama."

"Leave a small amount of food in your plate."

"Okay, Mama."

"Okay, Leo." She reached up to squeeze my hand, eyes closed, and almost smiled.

E.B. gave me shoe polish he'd kept in his closet since before he'd lost his legs. I took off my sports coat and polished my shoes while drinking beer. E.B. drank beer too, and said a blind man could polish better. The sun was sinking, but it wasn't gone, and E.B. tried to coach me into not being nervous.

"Their shit stink too," he said. "Bad as yours."

"I'm not nervous," I said, and drank another beer to make the lie come true.

"Trick is to look 'em in the eye, and make sure they be the first to look away. Same way you train a dog. Don't let them intimidate you."

"You've said that before."

"You don't listen sometimes. "

Polished my other shoe and drank another beer and left, feeling nervous. Spent forty-five minutes in the Winn-Dixie wine aisle, taking bottles off the shelf and putting them back again, studying price tags and years. A '99 Chardonnay was the most expensive I could find— $13.95—so that's what I bought, along with a six pack of Old Milwaukee, because it goes down like water, and six beers could easily be consumed in the fifteen-minute drive. Hoped I wouldn't have to open the wine. Kate had me open a bottle once, and I splintered the cork, pushing it down into the bottle. We poured through a colander and spit out wooden crumbs.

What I *did* have was a brand new car. My brand new car allowed me to suspend the disbelief that I was not indigenous to Sea Island. Thought when

I drove down the Sea Island causeway and then down Sea Island Dr. without being noticed, that I would feel indigenous. Looked into each car and saw that they weren't looking at me. Their not looking at me meant they weren't surprised to see me there. Took joy in their not looking, but still didn't feel indigenous. Drove past thirty-five streets, many named for Indian tribes, turned right on the thirty-sixth, and instantly saw the ocean over a wall of rocks. Rolled down my window and listened to my wheels crush oyster shells. The driveway stopped at the wall of rocks. Finished the sixth beer, popped a Certs, and left my car. Walked against a strong breeze with fat and salty fingers. It might have been a wind. A mild wind with skinny hands. It could be said that the air was moving. It could be said that the air was moving more than I'd felt the air move in a long time, and inside the air, certain healthy ingredients were being thrown about. It was the kind of air nice people might call nice. Squatting fat above the ocean was the kind of moon nice people might call pretty. Pairs of little lights were planted inside the lawn, like the eyes of frogs, and when I walked past them, they croaked loudly, and signaled bright floodlights to shower down on the entire yard. Security frogs. Specially trained. Bullfrogs. Specially trained bullfrogs. Stepped between two white pillars and rang the bell. Eve soon pulled open the door, wearing a black evening gown, earrings dangling. She stepped to the side and swept her arm across the foyer, and I stepped in, handing her the wine, staring at her made-up face. She'd applied subtle textures of makeup around her eyes and lips. She never wore makeup to work, and I was surprised now, to see her looking so at home.

She smiled, showing me her imperfect teeth, and my stomach stirred with hope.

Soft jazz played above the murmur of distant voices. We ascended several steps and came into a high-ceilinged den with orange walls. Six people were gathered around an older man who held the remote control to a big screen television showing a fleet of cops chasing a shirtless man through a trailer park. Eve led me to the group of people, stopped behind them, and cleared her throat. No one heard. The older woman standing beside the man with the remote control complained that the music was too loud and she couldn't hear what was happening on the television. She slapped the man's shoulder and told him to turn it up, which he did, over the jazz, and soon the stomping feet and heavy breathing of all the heavy cops closed in on the room from a group of surround-sound speakers I couldn't see. The woman said, "It's like being right there in the middle of it." The man turned up the volume again, and nobody said anything for awhile while the chase continued.

Eve walked to the side for a better view, and I followed her. "What did this guy do?" she yelled.

No one answered her. The chased man threw trashcans into the path of the chasing cops, and loud explosions ricocheted first from the front left side of the room and then from the rear right side of the room. Thought for a moment that someone in the kitchen had dropped a tray.

"I said 'What did this guy do?'" Eve said.

No one seemed to know. The chased man rounded the corner of a trailer and smacked into a telephone pole. The five wheezing cops caught up with him. Four of them held his arms and legs while the fifth pressed a knee into the man's upper back.

"Got him," the man with the remote control said. "They got the son of a bitch."

"Thank goodness," the woman beside him said.

"They ought to knock the shit out of him for making them run so far," said the smaller man next to the man with the remote control.

Eve snatched the remote control from the older man and turned off the television, giving rise to the soft jazz again. The man gave her a blank and hurtful expression.

"I'd like you all to meet a friend of mine." Eve introduced me then to her father, and to her mother, and to her sister, and to her brother-in-law, and to her brother and to her sister-in law, and I shook every hand and said nice to meet you to everyone I met.

"His hands are cold," said Eve's mother, Estel.

"Must be nervous," said Eve's father, Fred.

"Bet he has a warm heart though," said either Eve's sister or sister-in-law.

Eve asked who wanted wine.

"I'll take a Bud," her father said. "And some dinner." He laughed at himself and the women filed out of the room, laughing too. Fred was tall and carried a substantial gut, but his missing teeth and suspenders softened a first impression of brutishness. His face was tanned from outside work. He was looking for the remote control. I'd seen Eve hide it on the mantel, but I didn't say anything. She put it behind a framed photograph of Big Dick and Little Dick standing on both sides of a shark hanging from its tail. The men sauntered around the room, as if inside a museum, careful to fondle every object. A sheathed sword hung above the mantel, and currently held their collective attention.

"Betcha that's straight from the Civil War," said either Eve's brother or brother-in-law.

"That sword's from the Revolutionary War," Fred said. "You can tell by the handle. See there how it's got that hand guard? What do you think—what was your name again?" Fred and the two men turned to me, but I wasn't looking at the sword. I was looking at another framed photograph of a man in a gray uniform propped on a sword— the same sword—I figured, that was now the object of discussion. Planted my hands in my pocket and said I wasn't sure.

"You're not sure what your name is?" Fred said.

"I mean I'm not sure about the sword, I mean."

The men seemed unsurprised. They moved around the room and fondled other objects. Fred picked up a ceramic Aunt Jemima, and laughed.

Estel brought Fred a Bud, and told him to quit messing with Mr. Taylor's things. "You're going to break something and cause Eve to lose her job," she said. "Dinner in five minutes."

Fred shook his big head and stepped across the room, motioning with his head for me to come with him. He opened a sliding glass door, stepped onto a wooden balcony and stared out at the ocean. I closed the door and stood beside him. We stood shoulder to shoulder for some time, saying nothing. A somber shadow glazed Fred's face, and I wondered what he was thinking. Wasn't sure what it meant yet to be invited here, where the only guests were Eve's family, though I was glad they were the only guests. They were not indigenous to Sea Island, and this made me feel more at home. They were hard workers who also knew little of wines and caviar. Couldn't help but place myself in the role where I was supposed to win favor with the father. I guzzled wine, hoping my nervousness might fade. Fred rested his meaty forearms on the balcony's top board and sighed.

"I'd give my left nut for a place like this," he said. "Listen at that ocean. Smell of it."

Listened and smelled. Couldn't enjoy it. The sound reminded me of cars speeding past our house while I sat with E.B. in our yard. And the salt air made me think of all the creatures—fish and shrimp—that were pulled, screaming, from their homes, and boxed up in subfreezing rooms by people like my mother who will suffer eternally from coldness.

"It's nice alright," I said.

"I've worked hard my whole life to have what little I have, which ain't much, and I could work harder, sleep three hours instead of six, but I still couldn't come close to being able to buy a view like this. What is it you do?" Fred turned his large head to me. His cold eyes were prepared to shift this way or that, depending on my answer.

"I'm a reporter," I said. "A journalist. Actually the Business and Religion Editor. Where Eve works. At the paper there." Finished my wine and looked at Fred, whose eyes had shifted into focus.

"Was that your picture I saw in there here a while back?"

Nodded and looked back toward the ocean, worried how Fred might have interpreted my smile, though I was also suddenly relaxed. I'd been recognized, and by all definitions that meant my stock was rising.

"I betcha Dan Rather and them guys started out just like you," Fred said. "And look at them, knocking down a few mil a year. Time you get that high, you might be making twice as much.

"I doubt that," I said, a bit too quickly. "I'm in the process of resigning." Thought I might've seen something in Fred's eyes that invited a confession. Thought I saw him take a deep breath and show some confidence that I might be trusted with his daughter. Thought I heard him ask me a deep dark secret.

"I'm not getting bogged down in a career," I said. "Especially a career like this—we do Sunday School stories that cram the warm fuzzies down our throats and make it too easy for us to feel good about ourselves—boy scouts who are organ donors—did you see that one? How about the love that oozes for the retard? United Way volunteers building swing sets and bank presidents planting trees. Not that it's different anywhere else. We might start out with good intentions, but if we do our jobs, it means we'll soon be absorbed in the process of making readers stupid. Information is not knowledge, Fred. The truth cannot be quoted. I think sometimes, Fred—

I think sometimes it's better to be illiterate. I haven't read a newspaper in months. If I read newspapers, it'd mean that I might come to believe that what's good for the powerful is also good for the powerless, that those who make the rules keep the powerless in mind. But the job of these papers is to keep us believing that we're in charge—people like you and me, Fred—working people like you and me who can answer a poll, and argue passionately about the price of gas. All I do is manufacture consent for the bewildered herd, as Chomsky says, citing Lippman. But the herd is too nice, Fred. There's too much nice news about too many nice people. What we need are more stories that capture evil. The Devil is the greatest teacher, Fred. In fact, I'd like to do a story on you, Fred. Could I do a story on you? I want to do a story about people who work too hard. I'm sorry. I'm talking too much. I'm out of line. You need another Bud, Fred? Can I call you Fred? I normally don't talk so much, Fred. Let me get you another Bud." I looked at Fred, and then at my own empty wine glass and back to Fred.

Fred squinted one eye at me—the same one-eyed squint I'd seen his daughter use.

"I'm not sure what all the hell you just said," he said. "And I'm betting you don't know either, but if I had to guess, it sounds to me like you're just plain lazy. If that's the case, I'd recommend very highly that you not have nothing else to do with *my* daughter. In fact, my feelings wouldn't be hurt none if you decided to walk down those stairs there and drive on away out of here. Let me make it a little clearer for you. If you never see my daughter again, I'll never break your neck." Fred squinted at me while he lifted his Bud and drained it. When he lowered the bottle he stood there a moment longer, staring at me, and then turned to go back inside, sliding closed the door behind him.

Turned toward the ocean, feeling foolish. Thought I'd heard Fred complaining about a life lost to labor, but what I'd heard, I realized now, was sorrow that he hadn't worked harder to afford a better view. Stared at the ocean, wondering what to do. From where I stood, the moon looked hospitable. Imagined a familiar crater holding a pillow and blanket just for me.

In another minute, Eve came out, carrying two glasses of wine. She gave me one, and said, "I see you brought out the best in my father."

"I talked too much," I said.

"I didn't invite you here so you could meet them. I asked you here so you could see Mr. Taylor's place, and so we could spend some time together after everyone left. Maybe you'd better leave for now, though, and come back another time."

"How about two hours?"

"Better make it three. It takes them a long time to eat."

Drove off of one island and onto another, circling. Stopped at "the village," where tourist shops sold inflated knickknacks—miniature lighthouses, seascapes, and bleached sand dollars—and where bright bars played beach music and sold watered down drinks. Claimed a corner barstool, and repeatedly spilled my drinks when nearby couples tried to hug and dance. College girls screamed when they recognized someone from a previous summer. They screamed OH MY GOD, and bumped into my back while hugging (spilling my drink), without apologizing. The college boys pushed each other as a gesture of friendship. They pushed each other into me, and I spilled my drink again. Spent thirty dollars on bourbon and watched the clock. Listened to the house band play Jimmy Buffet songs. Several couples—maybe honeymooning—sang loudly, and off-key. They sang of cheeseburgers in paradise, and lost shakers of salt. Between songs, they kissed sloppily, and I was not jealous. One man pressed against me while waiting for drinks and asked me where I was from. I imagined he'd seen me alone, and pitied my solitude. He wore a button-down short-sleeve shirt with a t-shirt underneath, which was a uniform of sorts, I'd noticed.

"Milton," I screamed at him.

But he hadn't heard. Screamed it again.

"Right," he said. "Is that the place that stinks?"

"Paper mill," I said.

"Yeah," he said. "We had to go through that place to get here."

Told him I was sorry.

But he hadn't heard. He scooped up his drinks and walked away.

In another hour, I got up and worked my way through the crowd, pulling on my coat sleeves. Said excuse me and pardon me to every group I walked through, and several times had to tap people on their shoulders so they would create a path. Still, they barely moved. Most of the time I had to tap them on the shoulder more than once, and say, again, "Excuse me."

16

Eve took a bottle of wine—a different bottle of wine than the one I brought, I noticed—and led me upstairs to a bedroom, and then to a spiral staircase that took us to the carpeted roof. We sat in cloth-lined chairs beneath the moon and stared at the starry sky. The breeze blew our hair and the dark ocean crashed against the rocks. Eve filled a wine glass and passed it to me, and then she filled one for herself. She said nothing commonplace about the view. She already seemed to think the view was common.

"This is nice," I said. "Pretty. A nice, pretty view."

She pulled a joint and a lighter from the pocket of her shorts, shook her head to move her hair, and then lit the joint, hands cupped.

"My parents," she said, blowing smoke. "I love them and all, but they drive me positively batshit, you know?"

"I do. I know. I do know. Yes. Clocks and calendars. They worship clocks and calendars. Quentin Compson's grandfather gave him a watch once, but he said I give you this watch not that you may remember time, but that you may forget it. Of course you see where it got him."

"I'd like to do something sometime that would shock them shitless."

"He killed himself—Quentin, I mean, not Faulkner."

"I've done several things they disapproved of—piercings, tattoos, pregnancies—but I'd like to do something really over the top, you know?" She passed me the joint.

"Though it might be argued that Faulkner didn't not kill himself, so fond as he was of the juice. Most notably corn liquor."

"I sort of wish I was a lesbian. They'd hate that."

"Faulkner may have wished the same."

"Maybe I could marry a vagabond. Are you a vagabond?"

"I'm not sure I'm qualified. What're the qualifications of a good vagabond?"

"A good vagabond must be prepared to go skinny-dipping at a second's notice without a second thought." She stood up and finished her glass of wine.

"A second thought?" I said.

And then I couldn't find her.

And then she was back on the roof, dropping a thick towel on me. Got to my feet, holding joint in mouth, and poured myself another glass of wine. Then I followed her, carrying joint and wine and towel. She led me down the spiral staircase and through the bedroom, and down the hall to another spiral staircase and down the staircase and through several interlinking rooms to a balcony and then down the balcony and down a narrow trail that wound around several dunes and head-high weeds and over a wooden bridge that went over the wall of rocks and landed us on the beach, which is where the ocean was.

She reached for the joint, hitting it deeply one last time, and passed it back to me. Then she dropped her towel and sprinted to the water, high-stepping until she was far enough in to dive. I stood on the high end of the beach, smoking what was left of the joint, and drinking what was left of my wine, for fear of wasting and wanting not, and because both of them were free. Eve's head surfaced and went under again and surfaced again. She didn't yell for me to join her and she didn't look in my direction. She seemed, in fact, to have forgotten me. I started growing lonesome. Finished my wine and hit the joint until it burned my fingers. Took off my clothes and stacked them, and made my way gingerly to the water. Very stoned. Feared death by drowning. But the fat moon was there, and as long as it stayed in view, I knew I wasn't drowning. Eased carefully into the water, stepping over breaking waves. Shuffled my feet through the sand until the water was at my neck. The water was too cold, and I imagined dirty things clinging to my skin. Imagined fatal infections induced by ingesting brackish water. Felt a violent thump against my leg and instantly saw the shark featured in the photograph with Big Dick and Little Dick, and so I screamed, but then Eve came up beside me and draped her arms over my shoulders.

"Scare you?"

"Not in the slightest," I said.

She kissed me then, moving her hands over my body, which was underwater. She clutched my erect penis and worked her tongue inside my mouth. My feet moved unsurely in the moving sand. A wave came over us and filled our mouths and was gone again. Couldn't find the moon and then I found the moon again. Then Eve dove quickly and I couldn't find Eve again. She surfaced near the beach and walked out of the ocean, running across the beach and toward her towel. Moved weakly through the water and the sand, moving opposite the moon and crossed the bridge and followed the path toward the lighted house ahead. She wasn't on the balcony or in the high-ceilinged den, so I moved through the house looking for her, tracking sand across the carpets, dripping brackish water and shivering from the bones. Too many rooms. Found myself next to the island in the kitchen where there hung pots and pans and cutlery. Searched the refrigerator, and found five brands of imported beer. The beer from the golden bottle didn't suit me, so I replaced it and tried the beer from the green bottle, which didn't seem right either, so I tried a different golden bottle and decided it would do. Went through the nearest door. Entered a deep cubbyhole with a concrete floor and high shelves on each side; picnic table in the middle, every square foot holding full liquor bottles. A full colony of full liquor bottles. Couldn't see them all. Wondered how I'd ever make a choice. The nearest portion of the nearest shelf seemed reserved for Scotch, and beyond them were a half dozen bottles of Crown Royal still in purple bags, and beyond them was a case of Cuervo Gold and beyond the case of Cuervo Gold was a sea of Absolut Vodka, and beyond the vodka, I couldn't see too well. Walked in deeper, over a case of tonic water, and stood over the picnic table, trying to decide. Thumbed through various gins and rums and whiskeys and bourbons. Needed caffeine to combat the drowsiness from the pot. Coke and Crown. But the Crown was too far away, so I reached into the center of the picnic table for Canadian Club and knocked a bottle of Cognac to the floor. Said oops. Reached for another one. Took it to the kitchen, got a glass and poured it full of ice and C.C. and Coke. Feet sticking to the floor. Noticed I was naked. Left my clothes on the beach with Big Dick's towel. Took my drink across the kitchen toward another door, feet still sticking. A trail of blood followed me. From my foot, I guessed. From the broken bottle I broke and then stepped on, I guessed. Left foot, maybe. Maybe right. Searched for a towel and then gave up searching. Keep the limb elevated, they say, in times of bleeding limbs, so I raised the toes on both feet, walking on my heels in search of Eve, who would certainly possess among her knowledge the location of a towel. Through many rooms that looked the same: dens and living rooms and dens of plush carpeting and antique furniture and bookshelves that held porcelain knickknacks and painted plates stood on end. And then I was in a room where the high ceiling opened to the second floor and I faced a wall of glass that faced the ocean, though all I could see was light reflected from a bulbous chandelier. Couldn't see the ocean. Or the moon. Sipped my cocktail anyway. Sipped my cocktail in honor of what I could not see. Sipped my cocktail and looked to the wall on my right, where slanted words were painted in fancy scroll. Squinted, but couldn't read. Backed up for a broader view. Didn't help. Went closer and took one letter at the time until I connected them to a word and then connected words. Seemed to be part of the poem from Sidney Lanier about the county's marshes. Same poem Sandy the Sand Dollar recited to me in part some nine months before. The word myriad was painted on Big Dick's wall. Someone calling. From behind and above at once. Turned a circle and called back. Turned another circle. Discovered an indoor balcony where there appeared a woman who looked like Kate, though it wasn't Kate. Looked at the balcony and wondered how one might get to it.

"You're naked," she said.

"I've sustained an injury." I pointed to my right foot. And then my left.

"Take the spiral staircase in the corner," she said.

Spied the staircase, wound tightly with carpeted steps and a thin metal railing. Held to the railing as I wound the spiral staircase.

"I am approaching," I said. "I am Duchamp's nude descending the staircase, except that I am not descending."

Came into the loft, furnished like a hotel room—chairs and table on one side, bed in the middle, private bath on other side. Sat on the bed and fell back, balancing drink on chest. Raised my foot above my head toward Kate, who wasn't there. Then she was there, with a towel, like I knew she would be.

"Other foot," she said.

Raised my other foot, and sipped from my cocktail glass.

"Did you bleed all over the fucking house?" she said.

"Only in the places where I walked."

"Despicable."

"I'll get it in the morning. Spic and span like new."

"Where's your towel? Did you leave your towel on the beach?"

"I left my towel on the beach."

"Fantastic."

"Could we make love now?"

"That's not going to happen."

"I'll suck your toes if you suck my toes."

"Go to sleep."

"I'm a little ticklish on the soles of my feet, but my toes aren't ticklish at all."

"You're sleeping here and I'm sleeping on the other end of the house and in the morning you're waking up and going home."

"Can we make love in the morning too?"

"Nope."

"I like making love in the mornings."

"If you need to puke, the bathroom's to your right. I'm leaving that light on and turning this light off."

"I also like making love in the afternoons."

"I'm leaving now."

"And of course at night. I'd have to say those are my top three favorite times to make love—mornings, afternoons, and nights. What are your three top favorite times to make love? Are you there? Don't leave, Kate. I'll be good. You don't have to suck my toes if you don't want to. Kate?"

17

The following Monday, when I moved my half-moon magnet from out to in, Eve gave me a professional and neutral smile, but did not speak. I tried to think of something sincere to say. Wanted to apologize. She answered her ringing phone and looked me in the eye.

"Good morning, *Coastal Georgia Sun.*"

"I'm sorry," I said.

"One moment please."

"I'm real, real sorry."

She answered her phone again, and said the same thing again, looking me in the eye again.

"Can we talk later?" I said.

"I'm sorry," she said.

"I'm so sorry I don't know what to say," I said.

She looked me in the eye and listened to a subscriber who seemed to be voicing a complaint.

"I'm so sorry," Eve told the caller, inflection so exaggerated I knew she was mocking me.

Walked away, and when I reached the stairs, I heard her say, "One moment please," but her voice again was so acquiescing I knew it was not for me. Stepped into the dim and dank newsroom, and settled at my desk. Mark and Mary Kay were already speaking too enthusiastically into their telephones; Little Dick Taylor was talking back to the AM radio talk show. Doris and Eula talked too loudly to one another about a beautician's schedule, and Orville was mumbling to himself about the Braves. Picked up my phone and dialed Eve's extension.

"Good morning, *Coastal Georgia Sun,*" she said. "Could you hold please?"

Said I could. Doodled over April, and listened to the programmed ads advertising the rates of advertising.

"Thank you for holding," she said. "How may I direct your call?"

"It's me. I just—"

"I'm sorry?"

"Leo."

"Sorry?"

"Leo Gray."

"Sorry Leo Gray? The asshole that owes me $300 for a carpet shampoo and $50 for a replacement bottle of Cognac, and $60 for a cotton beach towel that disappeared? That sorry Leo Gray?"

"Do you really think he'll miss the—"

"I'll be happy to accept a check, today before noon, please."

"Would you like to have lunch?"

"If it helps you to live with yourself, I'll accept your apology with receipt of your check, before noon, at which point we can proceed with our professional, but not personal, relationship. If you refuse to these terms, I'm afraid I'll have no choice but to inform Mr. Taylor how you damaged his property and possessions, at which point I'm sure he'll see fit to terminate your position. I can't tie up the line anymore. Sorry." She hung up.

Doodled over April.

Mary Kay said, "Oh my goodness," into her telephone. "How horrible."

Mark said, "You still owe me three dollars, Buck—you cheap son of a bitch."

Little Dick Taylor called me to his office, and I went there dutifully.

"We're having lunch," he said. "Me and you and about fifty other people at the Chamber. You get a free lunch, and you get to write an article about the lunch, which is being given by local business leaders to honor local media."

Went to my computer, and moved the flooding Mississippi to the Altamaha River, where only those already living in moored houseboats had survived.

Went to lunch at the chamber and sat at a table with people I didn't know or care to know. Made it through the salad and entrée without having to return a single commonplace remark. Kept my head lowered to my plate amidst all the laughter and good cheer, and busied my hands and mouth with eating. During the meal, the itching I'd suffered throughout the morning grew more severe, and several times I put down my fork and scratched my chest and arms and legs while staring closely at a tiny chicken breast.

After dessert, a white-haired man in a suit stood at a podium and spoke of the gratitude the local business community owed the local media for having the courage to promote a positive image of the community instead of dwelling too deeply on the negative. He read from a list and called out a string of names: sales executives, producers and newscasters from Channel 2, the same from several AM radio stations and the same from the *Coastal Georgia Sun.* Each person took long strides to the podium and shook the hand of the man in the suit, holding it, with their smiles, for Lester, who crouched in the corner, taking pictures. A red-dressed lady behind the white-haired suit pulled framed certificates from a box and handed them to the white-haired suit, who then handed them to every person who came forward. The white-haired suit asked if there was anyone in the room he had inadvertently overlooked. A woman from an AM radio station raised her arm, high and mighty, flesh flapping. This was the same woman who would later be spoken of enviously by Mark and Mary Kay for landing a job in Washington as press agent for Rep. Jack Kingston, (R-Ga).

"Is there anyone else I'm overlooking," said the white-haired suit.

Slumped in my chair, carving the last corner of my chicken breast. Little Dick Taylor rose from his front row seat and whispered something to the white-haired suit.

"Of course," the man said. "We were saving the best for last. This award is the first annual Sidney Lanier newsman of the year award, which goes to the person voted the year's largest promoter of positivity. It goes to Leo Gray, Business editor of the *Coastal Georgia Sun,* who seems to be hiding in the back of the room there. Come on up, Leo."

Shoveled the last of my chicken breast into my mouth and scratched my chest.

The white-haired suit started an applause the rest of the room mimicked. I chewed a tough piece of chicken and scooted back my chair and walked to the front, scratching my stomach. Shook his hand, and received my certificate and didn't smile for Lester, who took our picture. Walked back to my table, saying nothing to all the people around me who clapped and nodded. Ate my last piece of chicken and scratched my arms while the white-haired suit offered closing words of praise. Walked out without a word to anyone, leaving my certificate in my chair.

On the drive back to my office, scratched my arms and chest and shoulders and my stomach and my legs. Looked to see if insects were crawling on my arms, and when I pushed up my sleeves, noticed a thick pattern of red bumps scattered uniformly. Went straight home, locked myself in the bathroom and looked at my body. Red bumps strewn across torso and legs. It was neither chicken pox nor poison oak. My genitals and my face were spared, but red bumps had multiplied everywhere, most of them capped with white. The small caps of white were in various stages of flaking. Was sure that I was dying. Put on a longer long sleeve shirt I could button at the wrists, and went back down the hall, not stopping to see mother, even though I thought I heard her calling me. Closed the door and stepped quietly across the yard to my car, hoping I hadn't woken E.B. Miller, who was sleeping in his wheelchair.

18

Went to the library to investigate my disease. A crumbling Victorian housed at the end of Worcester Street, past an out of business thrift store and a brand new city jail. The Downtown Rejuvenation project had lobotomized Worcester. The cobblestone sidewalk (furnished with candy-cane shaped street lamps, antique wooden benches, and synthetic-looking saplings) stopped at the new jail, where the last dollar of the already over-budgeted $5.4 million dollar beautification project was spent. The remainder of the old sidewalk had been uprooted and was now left in neat squares of dirt marked by small boards meant to hold concrete. The dirt-squared sidewalk dead-ended at the library.

Stood in the foyer of the library, trying to recognize the place in my youth that I'd called a sanctuary. All the windows were open, but the air was too hot to move. The wood floors were scuffed and splintered, and the pockmarked walls were missing paper. A single librarian, like a wilting great-grandmother, shuffled behind a long desk, carrying a computer. I'd hidden here after grade school. Took books to faraway corners and hid in cubicles so no one would see that I was reading instead of playing baseball in the park. The smell of all the books—though I didn't know then that it was the leather and the glue and the dust—had sedated me. That smell was missing now. There was something unpleasant in the air. Something clinical mixed with something florid. Thought of medicine floating down the hall of a crematorium. Thought of E.B. Miller's breath when I caught it sometimes in the early mornings. Thought of mother's bedroom at four a.m.

Scratched my arms and chest and followed the elderly librarian to a medical encyclopedia. Carried it upstairs, past an old man fingering white cards from a wooden drawer. Entered the rare collection room and sat at one end of a long oak table. A green cooking pot was centered in the table, catching drops of water from the center of a brown stain in the ceiling. Two tall windows were open, but there was no air.

Opened my medical encyclopedia, scratched my stomach, chest and legs, and thumbed through pictures devoted to diseases of the skin. Faces lost to acne. Torsos mapped in the purple lesions caused by AIDS. Holes in the middle of leper's faces. Moles stacked on the backs of necks like wild mushrooms. Pigment deficiencies causing splotches like spilled paint. Lower lips oozing cancers. Carcinomas feasting on the tongue. Clear mounds waxing beside infected ears. Genitals buried in pink warts. Clear blisters on red bases inspired by Herpes Simplex II. Yellow ulcers blooming between the labia and the rectum, planted there by Syphilis. Entire bodies smeared in scaling red. Red bumps capped with silver scales. Silver scales riding armies of red bumps. Red bumps and silver scales that wear the skin. Psoriasis. My disease. Triggered by infections, injured skin, changes in climate, stress, excessive alcohol intake, or sunlight deprivation. No cure, though treatment may enhance quality of life in this highly visible and potentially embarrassing disorder.

The book made no mention of specific stresses, and made no attempt to justify the need for excessive alcohol, or the rational for avoiding sunlight. The book said nothing about the specific stress having to do with insomnia, induced at four a.m., when the victim wakes to turn off the television of the victim's mother and can't get back to sleep and must stare then at the ceiling until daylight, thinking about the history of his thinking. Which is what I did. What I thought about in these hours was how I couldn't really think at all compared to the thinking I thought I'd once done inside my tollbooth. And in the silence of that hour, a kind of clarity swept over me and allowed me to see clearly all the maladies that visited me through the day, but which the day then made me forget when I was inside of it. During the day all the symptoms amalgamated into the general, and all I could determine was that I felt vague sickness. In the agony of the working day, all my senses grew too clouded to feel anything but sickness and dull regret, and so I often forgot the source of my unhappiness. Until four a.m. At four a.m. I recalled the precise pitch of the ringing in my head and how the ringing gave rise to constant headaches and how the headaches grew into dizziness and how the dizziness blurred all the objects of the world, and how all the blurred objects of the world made me feel as if I was sometimes floating outside myself, laughing at my own bloated body.

Closed the book and started at the beginning. Addison's Disease: a failure of the adrenal gland to convert carbohydrates into energy. JFK's affliction. Read about Addison's Disease and then put my head down to think about it.

Imagined holes in my stomach where food fell out. Then dreamed my father was standing naked inside a kitchen, commenting on the peculiarity of having a liver attached to the outside of his body. Dreamed I was at my father's feet, a full-grown kid, sifting dog food through my fingers. My father stabbed his liver with a kitchen knife and leaned over my dog food to drip his blood. "Stop crying," he said. "There's people starving in the world."

A line of drool hung from my mouth to the open book. Detached it with my hand, and watched it snap back into the saliva pooling on the page devoted to Addison's. For several moments forgot someone had woken me. A skinny man with a fat beard faced me, holding a folder beneath one arm.

"So sorry," he whispered.

He spoke with an accent I couldn't place.

"I normally allow our patrons such moments of leisure," he said, "but I'm afraid we have a meeting scheduled that will require use of the room."

The accent wasn't British and it wasn't Australian. I put up a hand and prepared to leave.

He stared at the green cooking pot. I sat on the opposite end of the table, flipping through my picture book. Neither of us spoke. It occurred to me, very fleetingly, that the library should have been something I should have wanted to write about. A drop of water plunked into the water collecting in the cooking pot. It plunked between us, but neither of us spoke. The man eventually left, nodding toward me. Stayed until he came back and told me it was time to close.

Bought the hundred and twenty dollar package. For this, I got eight treatments in the super ultraviolet bed, recommended by a dermatologist to arrest psoriasis, though all it did was increase the severity of the itching and the volume of the flaking. Waited in a lobby decorated with synthetic palm trees and a glass-top coffee table displaying magazines of the tropics. Watched clients come and go while waiting for the women who looked like nurses to call my name. People stormed in confident and triumphant, often whistling, and people left looking pink and drained of strength, searching everywhere for surfaces that would reflect themselves. The women who looked like nurses called my name from a clipboard and gave me towels and eye goggles and told me, for example: "room seventeen." Once in the room, I turned off the piped in music, took off my clothes and lay in the glowing bed, covering my testicles with the towel for fear of cancer. Lay there listening to the burning lights, smelling my own scorched skin. Each tanning session set me on fire, and the time between the tanning bed and a cold shower was equal to a season spent in hell. Took beer into the shower. Once showered, my scales glowed pink. The showers anesthetized the burning briefly, though it flared again as soon as my skin touched clothing or furniture. So I drank myself to sleep and woke at four a.m. on the vinyl cushions of the loveseat, coated in sweat and flaking scales. I took off the cushions and shook off the scales, and turned the cushions over. Listened to mother's television, but did not turn it off. And the next day, on my lunch hour, I went back to the tanning bed for more ultraviolet light, taking no pleasure in my tanned face.

On a warm afternoon in April, I sat unmoving in the metal rocking chair beside E.B. Miller, staring unblinking at a dying dog. Somebody's bumper had sent him airborne, and then I watched him bounce. He thumped his tail once, and didn't move again. E.B. Miller may or may not have seen it. Didn't ask. I'd been staring at the same spot in the road before the dog entered the picture, so I didn't have to move my eyes at all to stare now at the dying dog. Hadn't moved in a while. My skin burned and itched, but I didn't lift a hand to scratch.

E.B. was drinking beer and telling stories on top of the too-loud Braves pregame show tuned to WGIG, 1440 AM—Bulldog Country. I was drinking too, though the beer I currently held had gone hot from not being lifted since I'd seen the dog get struck. I'd been drinking beer for an hour since getting home, because I had to go back out again. Little Dick Taylor had assigned me to cover a dinner banquet at the Cloister on Sea Island featuring a keynote address by Barbara Dooley, wife of long-time University of Georgia football coach Vince Dooley, retired. She would be reading from her new book, *Confessions of a Football Wife*. And answering questions. Some of which, I was supposed to ask.

So I'd been drinking.

Judging by the lack of tonal shift in his non-halting speech, I guessed E.B. hadn't seen the dog get struck. A mutt, really. Dirty and skinny, and likely homeless. Probably a bastard mutt. E.B. was talking of the 1938 Atlanta Black Crackers. Drivers straddled the dead dog, not slowing. He talked of Gabby Kemp and Pee Wee Butts. The sky slipped into dusk. One season was bleeding into the next. He talked of Red Moore and Bullet Dixon. Fat clouds turned black and a strong breeze blew into our faces smelling of rain, but neither of us mentioned it. He talked of Joe "Pig" Greene and Felix "Chin" Evans. Imagined myself one year from now, sitting in the same chair, fatter, waiting for my next assignment, finding my art, finally, in telling time from the changing sky. He talked of the 1938 championship series played against the Memphis Red Sox, canceled after two games. The rain began abruptly, fat drops pounding the tin roof behind us like dropped nails. E.B. backed his wheelchair beneath the tin-roof overhang, but I didn't move. It came at a sharp angle, almost horizontal, pelting me in the face. It wasn't raining in Atlanta, some three hundred miles away, because Skip Caray came back from a commercial just to say stay tuned, it was a beautiful night for baseball. The dead dog was getting drenched. The dead dog's hair was matting up. E.B. turned his radio up over the rain. Zachariah Nebulous Linney said it wasn't his job to sell me a car; it was his job to help me make choices. The rain stopped as quickly as it began, and the sun came out again. The dead dog's hair glistened with wetness. E.B. pushed his wheelchair back out beside me, radio in lap, which he forgot to turn back down. To his credit, he said nothing of the rain.

Skip Caray entertained call-in questions from people who talked in a wide range of southern accents. Derek, from Selma, Alabama, wanted to know how come the umpire in his boy's little league game didn't award his little boy first base after his little boy swung at a third pitch that also struck him on the shoulder, and what would happen, Derek wanted to know, if that ever happened in the pros?

The screen door behind me closed and mother said hey to E.B., and wanted to know if he didn't agree that it was a quick shower we'd just had. E.B. said it was. I didn't turn around, but I knew she was in her bathrobe and slippers.

Skip laughed at the caller and apologized for laughing. Said it would be very rare for someone in the pros to swing at a third strike that also hit them in the shoulder.

"You could have smiled," she said to me. Heard her ruffling newspaper pages. "Look here, E.B." she said. "Leo got his picture in the paper for being named Business and Religion editor. He tell you he got promoted?"

"He don't never tell me nothing except my radio's too loud."

"He didn't even smile," she said.

"When you ever saw him smile?"

"He used to smile when he was a child. He used to smile then, sometimes."

"Them days dead and gone, honey," E.B. said.

Frank, from Ft. Sumter, said what ever happened to Chief Nocahoma?

"I feel like cooking us a little dinner," mother said. "A little celebration dinner. Leo, go to the store and get some things."

Skip said he guessed the Chief was back on the reservation, thank you for the call.

"I want some cabbage," E.B. said.

Mother said, "Go on to the store, Leo. Get some cabbage."

"And succotash," E.B. said. "Cabbage and succotash."

"And pork chops," mother said.

"I'm not eating," I said.

"You gone fry 'em or bake 'em?" E.B. asked.

"Get some flour too, Leo. We'll fry them crisp and eat them with our hands."

"Get some peppers," E.B. said.

"I'm not eating," I said.

"And some bread," mother said.

"Cornbread mix," E.B. said.

"Or would you rather have biscuits?" mother said.

"Cornbread," E.B. said. "Cornbread and maple syrup mixed up with butter."

"Better get some butter, Leo," mother said.

"Not eating," I said.

"What else?" mother said.

The voice of Zachariah Nebulous Linney once again came through E.B.'s radio, saying, "I don't want to sell you anything. My job is to help you make choices."

"Leo, get whatever else you'd like."

Gulped beer. "I'm not eating, mother. I'm going to the goddamned cloister on Sea Island to cover some goddamned boring-ass pitiful woman who has pitiful anecdotes to share about being the pitiful wife of a goddamn football coach."

Gulped beer. The dead dog hadn't yet been resurrected. The dead dog would soon be hosting ants.

A furniture salesman guaranteed I'd never move again.

"You don't have to talk to me that way," mother said.

"You ought to be taking *her* to the goddamned cloister," E.B. said. "Your poor old mother who you ain't never done nothing for except cause grief who ain't never seen the inside of the Cloister, I bet."

Gulped beer.

"I never have," she said. "I've seen the outside, but I've never seen the inside."

Little Dick Taylor had said I could bring a date, and I'd earlier asked Eve, but she professionally declined, citing a prior commitment.

"They only gave me one ticket," I said.

"Your attitude needs a little tiny adjustment," she said. "You think I'm in any condition? I saw your picture in the paper, and thought it might be a big deal, but it's obviously not. It's just about impossible to believe you're thirty-three years old."

Finished my beer and popped another, saying nothing. The sun rose higher and ruined memories of the rain.

"Let's us order a pizza, Miss Marjorie," E.B. said.

"I'm going back to bed."

"Last time I ordered a pizza though, they said they couldn't deliver out here."

"I'm going back to bed," she said.

"Like I'm in some condition to be cutting up the pizza man."

"I'm going back to bed."

The screen door shut behind me, and I sipped beer, saying nothing.

"You fucked up," E.B. said.

Gulped beer. A tractor-trailer crushed the dog and the dog's entrails leaked into the road. I rolled down my sleeves so the sun wouldn't reach my skin.

"Here you had your mama clean outside and all you do is drive her back to bed."

Imagined myself lying in a circle of a thousand people who had gathered to stone me with their voices. Voices came at once from every angle. There were the voices of co-workers and the voices of mothers and the voices from neighbors telling unending stories. Voices from ladies in advertising who talked of food. Choruses from the herd bringing business and religion briefs. So many unsolicited "thank yous," sung in cheap falsetto.

Giggling voices dominated the radio. Voices hired for the quality of their giggling. Giggling voices trained to increase the confidence of consumers. And when I went to the movies to get away from the voices, the worst voice of all appeared—the baritone voice dripping melodrama as he previewed all the voices yet to come. And there were the voices stupid enough to talk back to the voices, all in the tone of Frank, from Ft. Sumter, who squashed his vowels and twisted his syntax; mumbling through missing teeth. Toothpicks held between the gums. Moving down Wal-Mart aisles with the speed of seals. Imagined myself squirming on the ground, holding my bleeding ears. Salt of the, sweet salt of the, salty sweet salt of the, sweet salty sweet salt of the smelly earth, these folks I call my family.

E.B. said, "You ain't got a decent bone left in your body, I don't believe."

Didn't answer him.

"You used to be a decent kid," he said.

Didn't answer.

21

Stopped at a liquor store and bought a pint of Vodka for the ten minute trip across the causeway, and then I stopped at a convenience store for orange juice and a cup of ice.

"I got to charge you for the cup," the lady said, voice full of status. "On account of they take inventory."

Spent my last dollar on an empty cup, mixed the vodka with the O.J. and drove toward Sea Island. At the top of the first bridge I looked in the rearview at the smoke pummeling from the smokestacks. Adjacent to the final bridge were inlets reserved for yachts, and beside the yachts was a pier where currently a cruise ship unloaded tourists carrying cameras and large purses.

Took a left at the end of the causeway and followed a narrow road that wound beside the brown-gold marsh. In the deepest corner of the marsh, beneath a cluster of bent Oaks, shadows gathered like standing water. For a moment, I thought it might be beautiful. I was prepared, at that moment, to accept a pocket of natural beauty. Then the marsh stopped and there began a two-level shopping center featuring tanning salons, bridal shops, real estate offices, video stores and a seven-screen movie Cineplex. Went another mile and crossed a tiny bridge meant to separate one island from the next. An old black woman in a pink hat stood on the bridge, pulling a crab basket hand over fist.

The Cloister was housed down a road to my first left, but I went straight so I could finish my pint of Vodka. Passed million dollar homes and billion dollar lawns—-driveways curving around sculpted waterfalls. Caught glimpses of the private beach. Passed Big Dick Taylor's house, where I'd spent the night with Eve, albeit in separate rooms. Thought of stopping to see if he'd like a ride to the night's festivities; accept his offer of a toddy or two. Of course I'd have to introduce myself, trust that he'd seen my name in his newspaper. Drove past streets named for

Indian tribes, and soon found myself at the end of the road facing a security hut and a black metal gate. A uniformed guard stepped out from his hut and waved me forward. I backed up quickly, giving him the finger, and sped back the way I'd come. Lifted my cup and rattled loose the last piece of vodka-soaked ice. Heard a thud against my car and kept driving. Looked in the rearview, but didn't see a thing. Kept driving. Somebody's teacup poodle, I hoped, sporting a pink knit sweater, pink bow and pink pedicure. The dead poodle would balance out the dead mutt I'd seen earlier. Kept driving.

Parked in the parking lot farthest from the hotel, filled with the beat up cars of the hired help. Put one foot in front of the other down a cobblestone sidewalk, past a blooming botanical garden that emitted fragrances so powerful I had to summon all my strength to keep from being swayed. Past the garden, laughing couples played croquet on a wide green lawn, trading off wine glasses to free their hands. Ahead of me, men in tuxedoes opened car doors for couples who joined a swarm of bright voices that rang with compliments. When I reached the red carpet, I stopped dead cold in my tracks because it occurred to me that the teacup poodle could have been a child. Stared at my feet, seeing neat pools of blood spilling from the mouth and nose of someone's child. Saw its twitching hands and blue eyes turning cold and dark. Couldn't possibly see the face of the child and also move. People flowed around me and looked back. The women clutched the arms of their husbands, startled. Lifted one foot onto the red carpet and moved my other foot in front of the first foot, and then stepped, one step at the time, up the red-carpeted steps, scratching absently at some irritation on my chest. Followed people through the double doors into a high-ceilinged lobby filled with trees and ivory statues and some kind of waterfall in the corner, which flowed over thick green ivy into a wishing well. Moved my feet down the red carpet, pushing with the crowd. Voices came from everywhere at once. Single words without a context hit me from every angle. Someone said "darling," and someone said, "precious," and someone else said, "drab." Lowered my head, and scratched my arms.

Someone called my name. Took quicker steps down the hall to get away. Then a hand had me by the shoulder. The hand on the shoulder spun me, and when I turned, I saw the smiling face of someone I didn't know. A face I didn't think I'd ever seen before. He kept smiling anyway, seemingly desperate for reunion. He seemed about my age, and from that I surmised that he was one of those faceless bodies who traveled high school halls always in the center of groups while I traveled always alone, head pointed at the ground. His was one of the bodies that teamed with football players to annex wide strips of the halls, their shoulders sometimes clipping mine if my body came too far off the walls. He might have been the one who once slapped my face. Once, I was leaving the cafeteria while such a group was entering, and because I stalled their progress, one member of the group reached out and slapped my face. Then he pocketed his hands and waited calmly for me to retaliate. The entire cafeteria watched me walk away, head pointed at the ground. The person in front of me who now sang my name could have been the same person who once slapped my face. But I couldn't be too sure.

"Leo Gray," he said. He hadn't yet stopped smiling, even though the hand he held in the air hadn't yet been shook. I lifted my hand, and he squeezed it too firmly, taking too far his father's advice.

He started talking about himself. Watched his mouth move energetically, and heard his voice come out like a vinyl record on 78 rpm. But I couldn't package his words into anything coherent. He bracketed certain phrases with big smiles. Bright voices moved in waves around both sides of us, clipping my ears. He held up an expensive-looking camera strapped around his neck and leaned toward my ear.

"This is just a part time gig," he said. "I put old couples in front of the waterfall and snap their pictures for ten bucks a pop. I work full-time at Hancock Insurance, here on the island. We should do lunch. I saw your picture in the paper last week, and I said to myself, I said, 'it's a shame how some people lose touch,' you know. It shouldn't happen. I said to myself, I said, 'I need to call the ol' boy up and take him to lunch.' How about Monday? No, Monday's not good—I'll be in Orlando. I'll have my secretary give you a call. We'll go anywhere you want. How about Benny's Red Barn? Nothing but prime cut. What brings you here?"

Scratched my stomach, trying to remember what brought me here. He looked around the lobby for old couples and then back to me.

"I bet you're covering the Barbara Dooley thing."

Nodded. Scratched my chest.

"Lucky dog," he said. "I met her and Vince once at UGA. They're good people. You're looking good, Leo. Got you a good base tan working, looks like. You're doing all right for yourself aren't you? You got you a woman?"

Scratched my left side, and started to open my mouth.

"Tuesday," he said. "I'll give you a call Tuesday. We'll have lunch. Catch up. I see a couple of suckers, I mean victims, I mean customers I need to snag. Definite New Yorkers. Look at the yellow socks." He stepped away quickly, and then shouted back to me: "Tuesday;" a word that sailed seamlessly to the top of a room packed with people accomplished in appointment making. Found the red carpet and shuffled down a hall, bumping against the shoulders of men in tuxes. Laughter and good cheer scratched my inner ear. The rug was too thick and I couldn't breathe. Felt we were marching toward purgatory. Seemed to be sinking in the carpet. Seemed to be wading through a swamp. Heard stiff clothes moving on big bodies and all I felt was a primitive instinct to keep moving. We marched down the red-rugged hall through a door and landed in a courtyard surrounded by pillars and bright flowers. "How gorgeous," the voices said. We followed the red rug across the courtyard and up some stairs and through another door where the red rug opened up into a sea of red carpet stretched wall to wall.

A poster of Barbara Dooley was propped on an easel beside a grand piano. The crowd dispersed through a series of double-doors, knowing exactly where to go. Entered the door next to the piano and came into a dimly lit room already filled with crowded tables, polite voices and clinking china.

The Maitre D—a little child of a man—stepped from behind a podium and intercepted me, asking for a ticket. He was proud of himself, this little child-man, apparently having risen from the kitchen with ambition, biting the back of every boss until he alone had the power to correct the imperfect ambience of the dining room.

"I'm afraid," he whispered, "that if you can't produce your ticket I'll have to ask you to leave." He put his hands behind his back and lowered his chin, resolved.

Knew my pockets were empty but I searched them anyway.

All the fat people from nearby tables had begun to twist in their seats to stare.

The child-man lifted his palm and pointed his eyes toward the door.

There were simple things I thought I could be saying to help my cause, but they weren't in my pockets either.

Little Dick Taylor came up behind the Maitre D, moving his mouth around his appetizer, and said, "What's the problem, Clay?"

"There's no problem at all, Mr. Taylor," Clay said.

"You think we should call the cops?" Little Dick said.

"No sir, Mr. Taylor, I don't believe that'll be necessary at all, sir."

"I don't know, Clay. He's not very well dressed. No coat, wrinkled clothes, mismatched socks."

"Mostly sir, he's lacking an invitation," Clay said.

"Are those polyester pants?" Little Dick said. "Look at those scuffed up shoes."

"And no invitation, sir," Clay said.

"I forgot to give him one, Clay. Don't tell anyone, but he's actually one of mine. Here to cover the event."

"He didn't mention that, sir. All he had to do was tell me who he was." He looked at me with one squinted eye. "Why didn't you tell me who you were?"

Looked at the red carpet and scratched my chest, wondering why I hadn't said who I was.

"See if you can find him a coat, Clay. I'd appreciate it. You okay, Leo? You look a bit lost."

Listened to the laughter at a nearby table coming from big bellies.

"He'll be okay," Little Dick said. "Just find him a coat and stick him in the back somewhere. You enjoy yourself, Gray. I'm going to get back to my Oysters Rockefeller." Little Dick made his way back through a maze of tables toward the front and took a seat next to Eve, pointing over his shoulder back toward me. Eve tilted her head and laughed a laugh that rose above the clanking of silver at nearer tables. Clay returned with a navy sports coat and I put it on.

"Will you be needing two seats, sir?" he said.

The logic didn't register. I was one person, standing in front of the Maitre D, being asked if I needed two seats.

"Shall I tell the kitchen to prepare an extra entrée?" Clay said.

Didn't understand.

"Very well," Clay said. "I'll show you to your table." Clay walked me briskly between tables toward the back of the room. Every person at every table seemed to look at me as I passed, fat faces twisted in the labor of chewing, squinted eyes seeming to judge whether I was fit company. He led me to a table in the rear of the room, the brightest and loudest portion of the room because of its proximity to the kitchen. Three elderly couples occupied the table in silence, heads bent over bowls of soup. Clay left me at the back of two chairs, nodding, and then went through the swinging doors of the kitchen, where there came the mottled sound of a distant argument.

Couldn't decide which chair to take. Started toward the chair to my right, hopeful that the old woman to the right of that chair would be less inclined to talk. Then the old woman to the left of the chair on my left called out my name. I couldn't remember. Her face belonged to the countless faces I looked into on any given day and never saw.

"Hazel Higgins," she said. "From the library. Please, sit down." She tried pulling out a chair for me, but it was too heavy, so I helped her. All the old faces looked up. I smiled feebly and looked above them to find the nearest waiter bearing drinks.

"Mr. Gray is Business and Religion editor for the newspaper." But the kitchen noise seemed to keep anyone else from hearing. "Business and Religion Editor," she said again. "For the *newspaper*."

The old faces smiled politely and bent their heads toward their soup again.

"My husband," Hazel said. She touched the arm of the man beside her, but he didn't move. "Retired, but very active; I assure you. Plays eighteen holes every afternoon. And this is—" she introduced the others, rattling off names and vocations, though all I heard was the latter: so and so who sold office equipment and his wife who sold party supplies; and a man who sold medical uniforms and his wife who sold picture frames; then another man who sold Barca loungers and his wife who sold Venetian blinds. The Venetian blind woman heard her name and extended a long arm in my direction, wrinkled skin hanging from the bone, as if melted. Didn't want to touch her, but I did, diverting my eyes past her to her husband, the Barca lounge man, who was folding and refolding his cloth napkin.

"Quite a colorful group," Hazel said.

Waved a hand at a passing waiter who quickly disappeared.

"I'm afraid you've already missed the salad and soup, you poor thing," Hazel said. "You must be starving."

Waved at another passing waiter and was ignored again.

Looked at all the tables between my table and the stage, trying to find

Eve and Little Dick, but there were too many tables and heads and the room was dark. At an adjacent table, a waiter waited for a man's approval of a cork and then a sample. The man nodded and the waiter lit a candle on a tray and held the bottle of wine above the candle as he poured into each of eight glasses. Hazel pointed to the waiter and leaned into me.

"That's so you can see if there's any sediment in the bottle," she said. "The last time I was here I asked them why they did that, and that's what they said—to see if there's any sediment. I've never been much of a drinker myself. I was always afraid I'd take a sip of the wrong thing and do something foolish. Are you much of a drinker, Mr. Gray?"

"Not much of one," I said.

"I was never much of a drinker," she said.

Tried to meet the eye of the waiter at the next table, but his eyes were focused on the places where he could place wineglasses.

"I can't wait to hear Barbara read from her book. It was simply engrossing. Have you had time to read it?"

Watched the waiter nod at the table he'd been serving and walk back to the kitchen.

"Not yet," I said.

"I can't wait to hear her. I was going to suggest she visit our library while she was in town, but quite frankly, I'd be embarrassed for her to see the condition it's in. Do you remember the leak we had in the conference room that was being collected in the green pot we'd placed on the table. Well, that room has suffered several more leaks, I'm afraid, and we now have four different pots that must be emptied twice a day. It's quite embarrassing. I'd hate for Barbara to see such a thing. What would she think of us? Oh look, our appetizers are arriving. What nice timing—Oysters Rockefeller, looks like."

A white-gloved waiter removed soup bowls and set down small plates holding four oysters on the half shell covered with some kind of stew and something green.

"How scrumptious looking," Hazel said.

The waiter nodded to the empty chair beside me and said, "shall I bring another?"

The logic didn't register.

"Are you expecting someone," he said.

Motioned for him to lean closer, and he did. "Could I get a large glass of wine," I said.

"Any preference?"

"Just a basic, something sort of large and basic."

The waiter shifted his weight and looked at me, seemingly annoyed. "Would you like a basic Chardonnay, a basic Zinfandel, or a basic Merlot? Your entrée will be a Blackened Chicken Alfredo if that helps."

"That last one you mentioned. That'll be fine. Thank you."

Only Hazel continued talking, save small praises exchanged about the food and service. The old heads leaned over their plates and ate like birds, pecking at small bites chased by sips of water. A different waiter brought my wine. I took it straight from his hand and gulped from it. The waiter stood beside me, waiting.

"Seven dollars," he said.

Took another gulp before he could take it back. Leaned toward Hazel and tried to whisper soft enough for her alone to hear. "How embarrassing," I said. "I just realized I've forgotten my wallet."

"I forget things all the time," Hazel said. "Just this morning I forgot to close the lid to the washing machine, and my clothes sat soaking for several hours. Or was that yesterday? I think that was yesterday I forgot to close the lid. This morning it was—what was it? It was something else. I can't remember."

The waiter waited.

"Could I possibly borrow ten dollars until tomorrow? I could drop it by the library on my lunch hour."

"Will you be able to drive?"

"To the library?"

"I mean tonight. Won't you be impaired? I'd be afraid to drive myself—you hear so many stories. But I guess one glass of wine isn't too much for a person of your weight." She pulled her purse from the floor, put it on her lap and raked through it with both hands. Her retired, but very active husband lifted his head and turned to her.

"What are you doing?" he said.

"I'm loaning this nice gentleman ten dollars for a glass of wine."

The man leaned forward and looked at me, bottom lip stretched over top lip, cold eyes staring through thick glasses. "Does this nice gentleman have a job?"

"He's Business and Religion editor at the newspaper," Hazel said, "and a very nice young man who has simply forgotten his wallet. And I can't seem to find mine. Let me hold your wallet, dear."

"When's the nice young gentleman supposed to pay you back?"

"Tomorrow on his lunch hour. Don't be so untrusting."

Hazel's husband slowly withdrew his wallet and spent several agonizing moments flipping through his bills before handing Hazel a five and five ones, President's heads aligned upright. All the faces at the table who had watched the suspense unfold bent their heads toward their food again. I gave the waiter seven dollars and kept three—a start on fundraising for another glass.

Rockefeller's oysters were consumed in silence. Entrees were delivered—a tiny chicken breast beside a few green beans marinated in Grand Marnier.

"How yummy-looking," Hazel said. "I can't wait for dessert. Probably a chocolate mousse. It's to die for. I'll have to go walking in the morning."

Drank red wine and stabbed green beans. The woman who sold party supplies asked the man who sold Venetian blinds if his meal was to his liking. He said yes and asked the same of her. She said yes. Chocolate mousse was served and consumed and given a resounding round of praise.

The chair beside me went backwards and then came forward, filled suddenly by a woman who smiled at me, and then the whole table, and then back to me again. She had carried her dessert with her from another table, and continued to eat it. Didn't know her, but she seemed to know me, and so I tried my best to smile. She wore a velvet evening gown revealing a constellation of freckles across her cleavage. Hazel looked into her plate and didn't say anything, though I could feel her leaning closer.

"I saw you from across the room," the woman said, "and I told my table I had to come and say hello. So, hello." She laughed at herself and smiled at the old heads looking at her from across the table. I scanned the room for another waiter.

"You don't recognize me," she said. "I forget sometimes that people know me mostly through my work. It's Sandy. Sandy the Sand Dollar."

"Of course," I said. "Right."

Hazel leaned across me, and said to Sandy, "how lovely to meet you. I've admired your work from a distance now for some time. I think it's wonderful what you do, though I'm sure it must be exhausting."

"It is hard work," Sandy said. "But I love it. I think you have to work a job you love."

Waived at a waiter who stared at me and walked through the swinging doors to the kitchen, releasing another portion of the same old argument.

"I can't wait to hear Barbara," Sandy said. "Have you read her book, Leo?"

"I've read it," Hazel said. "I was telling this nice young man earlier how delightful it was."

"I can't wait to hear her," Sandy said. "I was lucky enough to be seated at her table. She's about the nicest woman I think I've ever met."

Stood abruptly and raised my empty wine glass at another passing waiter, who nodded back to me, and went into the kitchen.

Sandy and Hazel looked to the front of the room, where Little Dick Taylor was standing behind the microphone, clearing his throat.

"Oh Goody," Hazel said.

"There's your boss," Sandy said. "I was at his table too. A very nice man."

Watched waiters deliver coffee to tables in the front. Little Dick spoke with great inflection about the quality of the food and service, and said it was his pleasure, as a representative of our community newspaper, to host this evening's event. He shared anecdotes about going to the University of Georgia that made people slap their tables and laugh. Then he introduced her.

A waiter spread coffee around our table.

Amidst applause, I told the waiter, "I ordered a Merlot."

"Of course," the waiter said.

Barbara Dooley said, "I've just flown in from Athens, and boy are my arms tired."

Sandy and Hazel slapped the table.

"But seriously," Barbara said. "I'm delighted to be here in one of the most beautiful places in all the world—a place where Vince and I once spent a wonderful anniversary. Though he spent most of it watching football."

A waiter brought my wine and waited behind me for seven dollars. I bent toward Sandy's left ear, caught a whiff of her strawberry-scented hair, inhaled, and whispered, "This is embarrassing. I've forgotten my wallet. Could I borrow four dollars?"

Sandy motioned the waiter toward her, and whispered something in his ear. The waiter nodded and disappeared and Sandy winked at me. I tried to smell her hair again.

Barbara told a story about Vince's doggedness in courting her through college—they met at a sorority mixer and then he started attending her church and continued courting her after he graduated and began working as an assistant on the football team and spied on her between her classes. He took her to the Elks Lodge, and after some few weeks, during a Sunday drive, came to a parking place out in the woods, where they smelled heaps of dung from a nearby chicken pen. They had it rough there in the beginning. Not a pot to pee in. She was used to nice things, but he didn't make much money. And then she got pregnant—Oh it was rough in the beginning.

Finished my wine and searched for another waiter. A group of them stood against the back wall, spellbound, as Barbara spun a yarn dealing with the politics of the remote control. She'd had enough of it one day, she said. Finally, she threw down her dishtowel and stood between Vince and the television and said, "Play me or trade me."

Sandy and Hazel laughed and slapped the table and looked at me to see if I was laughing too.

"Isn't that funny?" Hazel said.

Tried to think of something funny, but there was nothing, and so I nodded.

Barbara told about the hassles of traveling, of people who came into their lives and out again, of Vince's bad moods after losses. She said, "Our lives were hard. But I'm here to tell you something. I'm here to tell you something through a song."

"Oh goody," Hazel said.

Barbara reached beneath the podium and pulled out a radio and a microphone. She placed the radio in a chair facing the front of the room, and pressed a button. The melody to a popular song started up—something I vaguely recognized but could not identify.

"I'd like everyone to stand up," Barbara said. She spoke into her microphone and her voice came through the radio, on top of the music.

Sandy stood at once, and pulled my arm so I'd stand too. Barbara started swaying to the music. She held her microphone with both hands and said into it: "I'd like you to hug the person next to you."

Sandy turned to me, put her arms around me and squeezed. I was surprised at the firmness of her body. I buried my nose in her strawberry-scented hair and closed my eyes.

Barbara said, "I'd like for you to tell the person you're hugging that you love them."

"I love you," Sandy said.

Her breath shot through my ear and bent my knees. I swallowed; said, "I love you too." I raised a hand and touched the skin above her dress and the room disappeared.

"I think you can let go now," Sandy said.

Barbara started singing over the music coming from her radio. She sang some lines that ran together—made mention of New Years Day and celebrations, and then she paused and sang, more audibly—

I just called. To say. I love you.

She put her hands together in a pseudo-clap and the rest of the room mimicked her.

I just called. To Say.

Sandy and Hazel clapped and swayed and looked at me to see if I was clapping too. Looked behind me to see if my wineglass was as empty as I remembered it being, and it was, and my hands, having nothing to hold, came together, clapping softly out of sync, though I did not sway.

I just called. To say.

Leaned into Sandy and whispered into her hair: "Would you like to get together after this lovely song is over and maybe have a drink?"

And I mean it. From the bottom. Of my heart.

"We can walk to my house from here," she said.

Leaned against the Maitre D's podium, close to the door, waiting for Sandy to stop hugging Hazel. Then I waited for her to stop hugging all the people she came across at all the tables between herself and the door. She kissed cheeks and held hands and cupped elbows, never covering her big-toothed smile, working the room with the grace and charm of a third world-queen.

She came to me finally, wrapped her arm around mine and walked me slowly through a maze of hallways and rooms until we found ourselves outside, near the eighteenth green of the golf course. Automatic sprinklers were dousing the green and parts of the fairway. We walked around a pair of sand bunkers and strolled beneath trees that lined one side of the fairway, Sandy's right arm locked tightly around my left.

"What a perfect evening," Sandy said. "Are those the brightest stars you've ever seen?"

The stars seemed out of focus, and so I nodded. Caught a toe in the thick rough and stumbled a half step before Sandy helped straighten me.

"Careful," she said.

"Yes," I said. "Careful."

"We're lucky to live here, aren't we?"

"Lucky dogs," I said.

We walked across a wooden bridge providing passage over a water hazard. I reached for the railing with my left hand, but there wasn't one, so I tightened my arm around the arm Sandy had locked around mine. We strolled down the fairway until Sandy steered us to the right, through a shallow grove of trees, stepping over above-the-ground roots and ducking beneath low limbs until we landed on her back patio. She led me around potted plants and small trees, past a glass-topped table and through a sliding door into her den. She turned to face me then, hung her arms over my shoulders and said, "Alone at last." She locked her hands behind my head and started kissing me. We couldn't find our rhythm. Her mouth was open too wide, or mine wasn't open wide enough. Maybe her lips were too thin. Or mine.

"You're a good kisser," she said.

"You too," I answered.

She called for her cat, Magnolia, who peered around the corner of the couch and bolted down the hall away from us.

"She's a bit timid," Sandy said. "I'll get drinks."

Sat on the couch, scratching my chest, and remembered my psoriasis. Wondered how to hide it if I should come unclothed. She returned carrying a wine cooler, placed it in my hand, and then she sat in my lap, straddling me, knees pointed to the back of the couch. She unbuttoned my top button. Raised a hand to stop her.

"We don't have to if you don't want to," she said. "We can take it slow."

"The lights," I said. "If we turned off them."

"If we turned off the lights?"

Nodded.

She turned off the lights and closed the curtains and came back to me. I'd unbuttoned my pants and lowered them to mid-thigh, positioned rightly, I thought, for her to sit again on top of me. She bent and touched it up and down, and then straightened and motioned for me to follow her down the hall.

"I need to hang up this dress," she said.

Shook my head, but she was gone and so I followed her. She'd already come out of her dress, and hung it up and turned to face me. I was already looking forward to the feeling I remembered feeling after sex, when for a few minutes the shape of the world fell into proportion and clarity introduced herself.

Sandy put her arms over my shoulders and started kissing me, and I picked her up, thinking it a manly thing to do. Picked her up and tried to carry her to the bed, but she was slipping through my hands and so I ended up half-throwing her, and then landed on top of her, bouncing.

"My goodness," she said.

Breathing too hard. Told myself to breathe, but I couldn't breathe. Hyperventilation around the corner. Had my pants down and was trying to push inside while I held each of her hands up around her head so she couldn't feel my skin. Feared she would soon raise the issue of safe sex and that the entire evening would collapse. Hurried to get inside of her, pushing clumsily against her pelvis while still holding onto her hands.

"Slow down," she said.

Turned loose one of her hands and reached down to guide myself into her, and then reached back to grab her hand, but it was missing, and then I felt her hand already under my shirt, roaming over the terrain of my splotched skin, and then I hurried to ejaculate, knowing that she would soon be repelled, but I couldn't ejaculate, and then her eyes shot open and she pushed me off of her and quickly turned on the lamp. Couldn't pull my pants up fast enough and all my scales on both thighs were now exposed in all of their red and white scaling glory.

"My God," she said.

"It's not." Couldn't think of the word that meant what I had couldn't be transferred to her. Fastened my belt and zipped my pants.

"You really, really, really should have said something."

"It's not—"

"I think I'm going to be sick."

"Three percent of the population has it."

"I'd like you to leave now, please."

"I'm sorry."

"Please."

"It's not—"

"Please." She covered herself with a cover.

Wanted to touch her, but she'd put the bed between us and I couldn't touch her.

Went out the way we'd come in, knocking against both sides of the hall. Went through the den and through the sliding glass door, and left it open so the cat could get away. Went around the patio and through the shallow grove of woods and down the eighteenth fairway, unzipping and squeezing to revive my dying erection. Stopped to concentrate, stroked, took another step, and plummeted into the water hazard. Enough instant clarity arrived for me to ascertain that I was drowning. My feet couldn't find the bottom, and I couldn't reverse the weight of my sinking head. There was time to think of a thousand faceless deaths. Legs above head. Or head beneath legs. Time to look through the black water and see mother's crying eyes, irretrievably ashamed, for finally having found me lying in a ditch. The world was upside down. Or right side up. Time to float into father's voice, which said, "You should have laid up, stupid." Stretched my arms above my head, or below, searching for things to grab. Pictured Kate sending regrets to mother for not being able to make the service because her boyfriend's diaper needed changing. Tasted black water and amniotic fluid. There was time to believe that I was as comfortable as I was ever going to be. Hand touched the surface of something, or the bottom of something—a rock or an egg or a golf ball. Pushed against it and found my feet beneath me, disappointed when I measured the water to my waist. Pulled myself out, slipping, sliding, and fell face first into the fairway. Picked a few blades of grass in front of my nose, awed by its general health, its bright greenness and uniform length. Wondered if I could order such grass for mother's yard—if they could deliver it and plant it for some reasonable cost. Started shaking with cold. Thought it'd be a good idea to get out of wet clothes and reduce the risk of pneumonia. Thought I should get up at once and run to my car and carefully drive home so I could be on the couch in case mother got up early and went to the kitchen. Thought I should summon every ounce of strength and get up real soon, before I fell asleep right there in the middle of the fairway.

Woke to the noise of a distant tractor, someone spreading fertilizer and pesticides in the middle of the night, or early in the morning. I was freezing with a teeth-clattering, arm-shaking, soul-jerking kind of cold. Stood and took off all my clothes except my underwear, balled them up and carried them beneath my arm the remainder of the fairway, around the eighteenth green, past the clubhouse and past the hotel into a series of parking lots, searching beneath dim street lamps for my car. Found it and threw my clothes in the trunk on top of golf clubs and art supplies. Climbed behind the wheel and drove off the island slower than I'd ever driven so no cop would have a reason to pull me over and see me naked and have the insight to question whether I'd been drinking. Drove into the newspaper parking lot without really knowing I was going to, though once there, it seemed natural enough that I should want to go straight into Little Dick's office and explain with exceptional clarity all the abundant reasons why I was now officially tendering my resignation. It seemed now to be the most crystal-clear bright-eyed piece of thinking I'd ever done.

Walked across the oyster shells to the double doors and into the lobby, empty, except for a fat woman at a desk in advertising, munching on a cinnamon roll while she shuffled papers. She looked up at me, mouth full, and stretched her eyes wide with shock.

She said, "Hell-fire sweetie, you done forgot your clothes ain't you?"

"I'd like to place an ad in the paper to sell my car."

"What in the world you done got into—poison oak?"

"Gutate psoriasis. Non-contagious. I'd like to sell my car."

"Psoriasis?"

"Non-contagious. My clothes are in my trunk because I fell into a ditch and I'm perfectly sober and I'd like please to put an ad in the paper to sell my car."

"Don't you work here?" the woman said.

"Until now, yes. I'm resigning. And selling my car, please."

"What you want for it?"

"I still owe over twelve thousand, so I'd like to just break even, or maybe even make a little money to retire on—lets say thirteen thousand"

"No, sugar—ain't nobody going to pay thirteen for it and it used when they can get a new one for thirteen-five. Me and my daughter—she just turned sixteen—we been looking for us a good deal all over town. You probably going to have to bite the bullet on this one, baby. Probably going to have to take you a little loss if you want to get rid of it at all. Course owing one or two thousand's better than owing twelve thousand. I'll write you a check right now, take it off your hands for ninety-nine nine, tag, tax and title."

"Keys are in it. Title's in the glove box."

She picked up her purse and removed a checkbook. "This is embarrassing," she said. "I can't even call your name." She looked at me and laughed, double chins bouncing.

Told her.

"That's right," she said. "I've seen you come through here about every morning, headed for the newsroom, and I've seen your name in the paper a few dozen times, and I knew who you were and all, but I just couldn't call your name." She wrote out the check, tore it and handed it to me. "I promise you that won't bounce," she said. "My daughter's gonna be tickled. I can't wait to call her. You want a cinnamon roll?"

Stared at her fat face a moment, saying nothing. Walked away. Descended the stairs into the empty newsroom and walked across the cold tile to Little Dick's office.

"I have some things to say," I said.

Little Dick jumped, and then recoiled, first frightened by the voice, and then the body. He saw me, his naked employee, sit in the lawn chair across from him, legs crossed.

"Good God all-fucking mighty, Gray. Where's your clothes?"

"I'd like to tender my—"

"What's that shit all over your body? You got chickenpox?"

"I'd like to—"

"Is it contagious?"

"I'm quitting."

"I'd say it's a good time. I'd say you'd better leave right now, in fact. I'd say you'd better go on up those stairs and never come back."

Had hoped.

Had hoped that when this moment came, my letter would be finished, and that after reading it, Little Dick would have no choice but to ask himself whether he too should quit. But I didn't have the letter. Didn't have a sentence. Had a pile of half-forgotten fragments conceived in daydreams. Couldn't even say now—couldn't even begin to say—couldn't even start to find a starting point to all the ample reasons why this job among all the jobs in the universe was the most evil job there could be.

Very tired.

Empty.

Tired and empty and dull and heavy and tired.

Very, very, tired.

"You have three seconds," Little Dick said, "to get out of here before I call the police, who can be here in thirty seconds."

Didn't move. Ground my teeth and stared at my young and stupid boss, waiting for the words I'd been waiting for.

"I'm not an appendage," I said.

"What?"

"Marx said we're just appendages of the machine. I refuse to be."

He reached for his telephone and I stepped out of the office. Then I heard him call my name and I stepped back in.

He said, "Did you write up the Barbara Dooley thing?" he said.

"I most definitely did not write up the Barbara Dooley thing. I am not—"

"Get out."

Left his office and walked back across the newsroom, past Lester, who had just stepped from the stairs, laughing hilariously while he raised his camera and clicked a single shot. Went back up the stairs and through the lobby, past all the other women in advertising who talked of flour tortillas. Eve had settled into her desk and so I walked up to her.

"I just quit," I said.

"I just heard," she said. "What are you going to do?"

"Don't know."

"Well, good luck."

"That the best you can do? Good luck?"

"It's short notice," she said.

She pulled out a magazine and started flipping pages. I waited three seconds for her to look up, and when she finally did, she raised both eyebrows so innocently that I wanted to rip up the circular desk she sat behind and throw it through the wall-length window. I wanted, after I threw her desk, to pick up every desk in advertising and throw them too. Then I wanted to get a sledgehammer or a chainsaw or a bulldozer. Eve still held up her eyebrows, giving me ample opportunity, it seemed, to list my grievances. But no words came to me.

"You realize," she said, "that you're only wearing underwear."

"Good luck," I said.

"And that you're completely covered in a rather revolting rash."

"It's not contagious." I turned and walked through the double doors into the parking lot. The oyster shells stung my feet, but I walked over them bravely, determined not to let anyone see me grimace. It was already very hot, and I knew that nothing in the universe would feel as good as the first sip of what would be countless beers. Looked forward to how the beer would eventually inspire sleep and how the sleep might eventually inspire some vague dream. It was just barely eight a.m., and the day lay in front of me like an empty page.

22

Couldn't move. Stream of light bleeding through the curtains and across the room, the only furniture. Underwater. God created caves. Couldn't scratch. Jealous statues. Dead memory. Envy the tongues of fish. Tunnels as far as the eye can see. Couldn't scratch. Just called to say. Just called. Just called to say. Called to say. God created caves.

Mother shuffled though a tunnel, slippers sliding. Pulled the curtain, said why ain't you at work.

Didn't answer.

You sick? Crossed stream of light. Sides of feet like a frog's belly.

Couldn't scratch.

Sat on loveseat, touching hips. Looked through window at shadows driving cars.

If you're sick I can call in for you.

Plastic trees.

She patted my leg, coughed. Said what's wrong.

Cardboard bark.

Patted my leg and coughed.

Yellow grass.

Patted my leg.

Yellow sky.

Coughed.

Yellow grass.

Went back through the tunnel, slippers sliding.

Ocean-colored asphalt.

Jealous statues.

Underwater.

Slept for days and woke up tired, drenched in sweat from dreams involving fighting.

Mother slid her slippers down the tunnel and pulled the curtains.

She said, "Happy Easter."

She moved my legs and sat, shoulders touching. Peripherally, the dark hall invited. Thought of going to mother's bed, curling fetally, sleeping away the day again. Stared through the window at passing shadows.

Mother said, "I'm going to fix Easter Dinner." A declaration meant to stir the ghosts.

Looked at me for reaction. Stared at passing shadows, saying nothing.

"I'm calling your grandmother and we're going to have her over. One big family. I've had a ham in the freezer for a year."

Scratched my chest, chastised myself for doing so and then scratched again more violently.

She patted my leg, went down the hall and came out some minutes later in a red dress several sizes too small, pockets of flesh pushed up around her hips and arms. She turned a circle in front of me, lifting her arms over her head, trying to twirl on tiptoes, losing her balance, and twirling anyway. Quarter-sized hole in her left armpit. Wanted to know how she looked.

Nodded once, and said very quietly, "Very nice."

She danced into the kitchen and started rattling dishes and closing cupboards. The noise of wars. Went outside. Sat in the metal rocking chair beside E.B., who sat in his wheelchair smoking his pipe, conductor's hat pulled low. Squinted against the sun and lifted the lid to the cooler between us. Found a stack of cans floating in wrist-deep water.

"You done stepped on your dick this time," E.B. said. "You ought to knew it was coming up on Sunday and stocked up. Got to go to Florida to get a beer today."

Sat beneath the sun, and grew a fever. Sweated. Searched my mind for a place where I might have hidden a beer somewhere along the way for a time like this when I badly needed one, but there were no such places.

"Done stepped on your dick for sure," E.B. said.

The sun rose cruelly, shining on the stillness. E.B. unwound a story about a long tradition going interrupted. Stared at the road and thought of hitching to Florida, though I wasn't sure whether the coincidence of Easter might change the law, making beer unavailable there too. The sun rose, and E.B. made noises in his throat to indicate he was parched.

In another hour, a white van pulled up. Then a white-shirted man led an old lady across our yard. He smiled idiotically, this man, and when they reached us, made unnecessary introductions. Met my mother's mother, again, and again, she said, "Pleased to meet you." Mother's mother was hunched so severely she could only see her shoes. She stopped at the door and asked whose house this was. White shirt said her daughter's. Mother's mother said, "Looks like hell."

E.B. pushed his one good eye away to discourage anyone from finding kinship. White shirt stood behind mother's mother, arms spread.

Hadn't seen her since some long ago Sunday when mother said we were going for ice cream and we ended up at the nursing home. Mother's mother had faced the window like a plant, not knowing who we were or where she was. Never went back, because what's the point in knowing someone without a memory? Tried to forget her, and it had mostly worked— a sign, maybe—that I was just like her.

Mother's mother gave white shirt a piece of folded paper and he read from it.

"You're on number two," the man said. "Number one was breakfast."

She looked at him, confused.

"Number three," he said, "is supper. And number four is to get a Snickers bar for breakfast." He folded the list and gave it back to her. He saw her inside without my help, and then rushed back out, across the yard and into his van, where he lit a cigarette and quickly drove away.

E.B. said he'd take his plate outside. I said I'd join him. We sat our paper plates in our laps, full of ham and potato salad.

E.B. said, "You won't find a *cold* beer within a hundred miles of us today. Me over here drinking water with my Easter dinner."

Put my untouched plate of food on my chair and walked across the yard and into the street, saying nothing to E.B. Walked all over town, looking for a beer. Passed churches, veering around boys with clip on ties and girls in pink dresses holding the hands of mothers and fathers who glowed because they knew the schedule for salvation. There was no breeze except for that created by diesel trucks delivering pines and stumps. Grew grateful for the diesel trucks because they deflected the noise of birds. Azaleas, simple hedges for eleven and a half months of the year, bloomed around the perimeter of churches, promoting false promises about enduring. Walked through the center of crosswinds blown from the paper mill and the sewage treatment plant, and lived for several seconds inside the Devil's asshole. Entered a convenience store to escape the smell, found wooden sticks slid through the door handles of beer coolers. Unsympathetic clerks read newspapers. Walked past dark saloons and barred liquor stores, past a street person who had planned ahead. Passed a clapboard house emitting the fragrance of someone frying chicken. Thought of begging for just one bite of a juicy thigh. Kept moving. Walked until I didn't know where I was, though all the houses looked the same. Trusted I'd find home by continuing to walk in circles. Imagined myself as my mother's mother, searching for bulldozed landmarks. Imagined myself preparing lists to remember meals.

1. breakfast.

No shade. Every angle of every house absorbed the sun and every small failure was illuminated—missing shingles, unhinged screens, cheap paint and untreated lumber softening on slanted porches. The sun shattered the veil of every house, and no one owned a mystery. On the islands, the ocean breeze sedates the sun. On the islands, colossal oaks filter the sun and scatter shadows across the sides of houses.

2. lunch.

Walked through the back of a dead end street, climbed a fence, crossed a ditch and found myself in the center of a dilapidated baseball diamond polluted with weeds and trash. Went through the outfield and through a grove of trees and came out in a cemetery of ancient headstones washed clean by rain. Plastic flowers decomposing. Corpses singing soft and low to be remembered.

3. supper.

Stepped in the center of a railroad track and walked between thick woods toward the setting sun. Slid through a funnel into the forest, darkening. Pockets of water gathered in pools at the edge of the woods. Heard a family of wild hogs scurrying. Passed the skeleton of an old truck, dull orange from rust. Sank into the smell of snakes. Stepped over molted skins. An alligator carcass, teeth intact. The moon appeared before the sun fell, and I walked instinctively down the tracks. Spied an owl perched on the low limb of a dead oak tree. Looked into his eyes and grew comforted by his wildness. Followed me by moving his head but not his eyes. Seemed to recognize me. Stayed in motion. Needed to keep moving until I arrived at some calm and distant place where I could sit in silence and wait for the resuscitation of memory.

4. procure snickers bar for breakfast

Left the tracks and walked through woods. My face collected spider webs, and my feet sludged through ankle-deep water. The sun disappeared and I couldn't see the moon. Walked through the deepest blackness of the deep black woods, limbs scraping against my cheeks. Collided with trees and felt my way around them. Choruses of crickets in numbers that could fill stadiums, croaked in code. Started to feel excited about the possibility of being lost. Started thinking how wonderful it would be to truly be lost in the woods, because that would mean that the woods might still be bigger than the world. Began to hope I would be lost inside the woods for miles. But the light came eventually, of course—too soon—the light of street lamps and houses and passing cars.

Found home by walking in circles.

23

Slept for days and woke in pools of sweat, mother's television in the distance. Stared at the ceiling and knew suddenly I was free to spend the rest of my life without speaking. This revelation moved me to my feet and down the hall to brush my teeth. It moved me to the shower, where I lathered a rag and wiped away the flakes of psoriasis that had shrunk and dried. It moved me to the kitchen to make a cup of coffee, which I was then moved to take outside, where I was moved, finally, to sit. Sat in the metal rocking chair beside E.B. Miller and squinted into the sun. E.B. Miller slept in his wheelchair and I rocked in my rocking chair to the rhythm of his snoring. Heard a woodpecker knocking on a rotten tree, and then remembered having dreamt of birds that had stood on my chest and stomach, plucking worms. Sipped my coffee and watched a tailless squirrel in the nook of a tree, rotating an acorn in black paws. Decided the tailless squirrel was the funniest thing I'd ever seen. Suddenly craved that someone else see it too. Yelled to E.B. that it was late afternoon, that he should stop sleeping his life away. He straightened his conductor's hat and pushed his body upright in his wheelchair.

"What?" he said.

I told him what I saw.

He dug out his pipe and tobacco from his overalls pockets, not caring about the squirrel. "Ain't you got a job you supposed to be at?"

"I resigned."

He packed his pipe and rolled up his tobacco. He fished out his lighter and held it over his pipe until it caught. I smelled peaches being cooked.

"It's a sorry man who quit his job when his mama ain't working too."

"If you had some money, I could get us some beer," I said.

"Listen at you. Out of work and gone to begging."

"We need about four dollars for a twelve of Hamm's and I have exactly—let me see—nothing."

"You sorry," E.B. said. He cussed to himself and reached inside his top overalls pocket, pulled out a wad of dollar bills. He twice counted three singles, ironing each one in his palm, and handed them to me. He unbuttoned a side pocket on his overalls, pulled out a handful of change and gave it to me to count.

"One of us got to get a job," he said.

I pocketed the change and walked toward the store, sweating within three steps from being fat and out of shape. My heart pounded and my upper thighs rubbed together. I put one foot in front of the other and looked up occasionally to see how much farther I had to go. The street was empty. The dirt yards of the housing projects were bare. People stayed inside, hiding from the heat. Opened my mouth to corral more air. When I stepped inside the convenience store, the cool air kissed me and asked me not to leave.

A large woman sat on a stool behind the counter, smoking, and reading tabloids. She asked me if it was hot enough, and I told her it was.

"You couldn't get me out in that heat if you was to pay me," she said.

I plopped the twelve-pack on top of a Help Wanted sign.

She took a final drag from her cigarette, mashed it out, and rose slowly to her feet. She was the largest person I'd ever seen. I tried not to look too directly at her for too long so she wouldn't feel self-conscious. Her skin was as white as candle wax, and she wore a white t-shirt as if to accentuate it. Her thick glasses stayed at the tip of her nose, and several pimples were clumped on her chin amidst a cluster of long black hair.

"You got the right idea," she said. "That's exactly what I intend to do in another couple hours. Comes to $3.88."

She unwrinkled the bills I gave her and counted out the change while I fingered the Help Wanted sign.

"You ain't got but $3.80 here, sugar. See if they's eight pennies in that thing there."

I scooped out three pennies from the red dish and handed them to her.

"Close enough," she said. She dropped the pennies in the drawer, turned the twelve pack on end and pulled a bag down over it.

"Yeah," she said. "Another couple hours and I'll be sipping on a cold one too."

"When are you needing someone to work?" I said.

"Soon as we can get somebody, sugar."

"I meant what are the hours?"

"Eleven o'clock p.m. at night to seven o'clock a.m. in the morning." She turned the beer back over and pushed it toward me. "You ever done this kind of work?"

"I've done similar, you know, working with people—about the same kind of work."

"It ain't too hard, but the nightshift, it's awful quiet. It gets lonesome sometimes."

"I don't mind that."

"Only pays $5.50 an hour."

"More than I'm making now."

"We been held up a couple times."

"You got to go sometime."

She smiled and pulled an application from beneath the counter. "Take this and fill it out and bring it back tomorrow. They just need a warm body in here as soon as they can get somebody. They been having to close here lately on account of they hadn't had nobody. My name's Gladys. I'm sort of the manager, I guess you'd call it."

"I'm Leo Gray."

"We'll see you tomorrow then," she said. "Try to stay cool out there."

I stepped out, tore the top of the twelve pack and opened my first, sipping while I pushed myself back through the heat. Thought of the lonely nights to come and grew excited. Thought of the years I'd spent in my tollbooth, legs propped, invisible to bosses. I wiped my wet forehead and cheeks with my long shirtsleeves and trudged back through the sun, thinking about the night.

E.B. said, "What the hell took so long? I thought you might have had the heat stroke."

I took our cooler inside, dumped our beer into it, and broke mother's ice trays over them. She coughed from her room, and I paused, but didn't go see about her. I took the cooler back outside and set it between E.B.'s wheelchair and my metal rocking chair.

"Don't be handing me one a those hot-ass beers," E.B. said. "Go stick a couple in the freezer for about ten minutes so they be good and frosty."

Did as E.B. wanted me to do and then returned.

"I just got a job," I said.

"Shit."

"Down at the Texaco Station. Graveyard shift, starting tomorrow."

"Sound logical. Go from being a editor to working at a gas station, where you can get your head blowed off any night of the week."

"Pays $5.50 an hour. I didn't think to ask about benefits."

"All the bullets you can stand. That's your benefits. Where's my beer?"

Retrieved a beer for E.B. and one for me.

"You better take my shotgun down there with you at night. That's all I'm going to say."

"No it's not."

"Better take my shotgun and shoot every customer who walks in before they have a chance to shoot you first."

I could sit undisturbed for hours behind the counter and stare into the night.

"Maybe you could get you a little handgun like a Derringer."

Sit and stare into the still night and never move, save the occasional customer.

"You can hide a Derringer in your pocket pretty good."

Sit and stare and never move.

"It don't hold but two bullets, but that's all you need at close range like that."

For hours at the time.

"One for each eye."

I gulped the last of my first beer and stared into the sun, thinking about the night.

"You might ought to go ahead and pick out a casket. Something cheap to save your mama some money. Maybe a nice wood casket."

I slept all night and most of the next day. I woke in pools of sweat and dry flakes of psoriasis. Went to mother's room to tell her about my job. Stood beside her bed, staring at her closed eyes. Listened to her breathing coming out like cracked whistles. Stood silent for a full five minutes, staring at the wrinkles on her face, waiting for her to open her eyes. Wanted to wake her and tell her not to worry, that I was working—that I'd pay the rent, and that I wouldn't leave her, and that I wouldn't put her in a home, and that I would spend the rest of my life staring at the night, thinking of all the things I hadn't thought to do for her. Suddenly wanted to get on my knees and hold her hands and apologize for neglecting her for so long. Stood there for five minutes, staring at her face, waiting for her to open her eyes so I could say these things, but she never did, and so the greatest gift I could offer was to leave her undisturbed. Tiptoed down the dark hall and walked to work. Sweat leaked from my head and thighs and chest. My long-sleeve shirt, worn to hide my psoriasis, was splotched in puddles, and my pants scraped painfully against my upper thighs. Pockets of flesh bounced as I walked over dips and rocks. I imagined myself growing into better shape. Entertained fantasies of jogging to work and then back home, timing myself with the second hand of a convenience store watch. Entered the final quarter mile, marked by the businesses that had failed as soon as the four-lane went through. What had once been a hardware store, and then a body shop and then a computer store and then a business called Office.Com was finally an antique store, now closed.

I walked across the convenience store parking lot, scooped up a piece of windblown newspaper and tossed it in the metal barrel between two gas pumps. Inside, the cool air bent my knees. Gladys looked up from a magazine, and said, "Hey sugar. You ready to work?"

I said I was.

"Well, come on back here and I'll show you where the stool is where you can sit when it's slow like this." She laughed at herself for a second and reached for her cigarettes. "It's been God-awful slow. About the only thing that gets me through the day is looking at these magazines. They's some dirty ones behind the counter, but most of them is wrapped up where you can't get into them. Last guy who worked the night shift, he'd rip them open and look at them and then staple them back shut. He got fired for not coming in when he was supposed to. That's about the only thing will get you fired—not coming in. You bring your application back with you?"

I told her I'd forgotten.

"Don't worry about it." She sucked on her cigarette and flipped a page.

I knew then that I'd probably grow to like Gladys more than anyone I'd known.

"I reckon you can start working the register a while so you can get the feel of it," she said. "It's a pretty basic register. All you got to remember is to punch in the amount and then what it is, like candy, or cigarettes, or beer, or soft drinks. Or gas. Go ahead and stand behind it. If somebody like me can run it, anybody can run it." She laughed at herself.

"Most everything in the store is already priced—I price things on Mondays after the groceries come in. The prices for beer and cigarettes is taped there on the register. Go ahead and ring me up for a pack of Salems. We'll start you out like that."

I hit the keys with one finger, going slow and easy for the sake of accuracy. Gladys gave me the money and I made change for her.

"You're a natural," she said.

Gladys smoked and returned to her magazine, content to set a casual pace for the time we'd take to get to know each other. I leaned against the counter and looked out the window to the dilapidated motel across the street I'd passed for two years without really seeing. It sat at the foot of the overpass, the final thing that went unnoticed in the long line of forgotten businesses and faded billboards before the overpass funneled drivers uptown and then to the resort island of their choosing. The motel was made of paneling meant to resemble cobblestone and every few feet a plastic green pole held up a plastic green banister. The doors and window trim were painted the same dull green— apparently discounted by the bulk. A group of Hispanics sat outside in furniture pulled from the rooms, drinking beer, and taking turns watching over a charcoal grill. A Gremlin with a head-sized hole in the driver's side window was the only car in the parking lot, backed between two sickly palms. Hooked to the upper end of the motel was a windowless bar called The Shipwreck Lounge. Atop a rusted pole was hung a Pabst Blue Ribbon sign, slumping at forty-five degrees.

Gladys tossed her magazine on the counter, mashed out her cigarette and looked at me. "It's not everybody can handle the nightshift. They's not too much riff-raff, but it gets awful quiet. You might go a whole night some nights not seeing a single soul."

"I don't mind that," I said.

"But they's not much riff-raff. They might be a few shady characters here and there, but they's not many will give you any problems. Except for Crazy Johnny. I'll have to tell you about him. He lives right over there." She pointed behind the motel where a narrow dirt road wound around some trailers.

"He don't mean no harm," she said. "Most of the time he walks around with his cap pulled down, not looking at nobody. Then I seen him other times when he's gotten all beat up. I asked him one time, I said, Johnny, how'd you get all them bruises, and he told me, he said, they just pop up whenever it gets cloudy." She stared out the window for a while, locking her eyes on some sad memory. "But he don't mean no harm."

A pickup pulling a cement mixer stopped in the parking lot, and a crew of workers unloaded themselves.

"Looks like a little rush," she said. "Reckon you can handle it?"

"I'll give it a shot."

"I'll be manning my position," she said from her stool.

They came in without saying anything, every face wearing death masks of fatigue, shirts and jeans drenched in dirt. Five men in a row bought quarts of beer, borrowing change from one another to meet the tax. They were in their twenties except for one ghost-thin man who must've been near seventy. The old man brought his beer up last, along with a loaf of bread, a pack of bologna, and a jar of mustard. He pointed to a generic brand of cigarettes, saying nothing. I bagged it all up for him, saying thank you, but he didn't respond. He walked out, climbed over the tailgate of the truck, leaned against the wall of the bed, and closed his eyes.

"Nothing to it," Gladys said.

I looked forward to having the place to myself. I spotted a low-sitting kitchen chair in the corner next to a five-gallon bucket I could turn over for a stool, and knew it was all the furniture I would ever need.

Gladys pulled a bag of M&M's from a display rack, opened them with her teeth, and sighed.

"I ain't felt worth a damn in three days," she said. "My mama's got a case of distemper or shingles one, and my hip's been hurting something awful back from when I got run over."

"You got run over?"

"In 1980." She popped some M&M's into her mouth and looked out the window. "The doctor had told me to get some exercise, so one night I walked to the grocery store instead of drove like I'd normally do, and this guy ran off the road and run right over me and never even slowed down. I got drug about a hundred yards. My face near-bout got torn off on the asphalt, and my hip, it was just hanging on by a thread. The doctor said I'd never walk again, but I said, you watch. I was paralyzed two weeks in intensive care. In fact, I'd never seen my daddy cry till the day he come in there and looked at me, and then he went to sobbing like a baby. I had to have a colostomy—you know where they put the bag on your side where all your stuff goes. Worst thing was they wouldn't let me have a cigarette or nothing for three whole weeks. When I finally got out, that first cigarette—it tasted terrible. That's when I should have quit, I guess, but I didn't." She reached behind her then and grabbed her pack.

"The Sheriff, he finally caught the guy. Tracked him down from car parts that was knocked loose. We went to court, and he sat up there and said it was a animal he thought he hit. Can you imagine any animals around here big as me? The judge knew his family and all and talked about how he was going to college, so he just gave him a little fine and let him go. His mama was setting there behind him during the whole thing, patting his shoulder, telling him everything was going to be all right." She put out her cigarette and stared out the window.

I didn't know what to say. I searched my mind for some similar experience I could share for the sake of empathy, but all I could think of was what had happened a few nights before, when I myself ran over whatever it was I ran over the night I drove around drinking the last of my drink before having to cover the dinner banquet on Sea Island. But I didn't know how to tell it properly—how to tie in the dark mood hanging over me at the time, and the powerful numbing dread I felt about attending a dinner banquet with people who would chortle at every anecdote of Barbara Dooley's imperfect life— and how, after that night, I sat for hours in a paralyzed stupor. I didn't know how to tie it all together, so I let the moment pass, pausing to honor her pain.

A man driving a green Saab convertible pulled into the parking lot and came inside, asking directions to Jekyll Island. Gladys pointed to the overpass, and then he pointed too, and the man said thank you, and Gladys said, yep, and then the man walked back out and unlocked his Saab and climbed in next to his frowning wife.

"You get that all the time," Gladys said. "The tourists will be cruising along and all of a sudden things won't be looking right, and they'll get a little nervous and come in for directions."

"I think I might pretty much have the hang of it," I said. "In case you want to leave early. You know, in case you're not feeling well."

She looked at me strangely then, cocking her head.

"Really. I think I can handle it. Plus, you need to be back here early tomorrow, don't you?"

"Six-thirty a.m. in the morning," she said. "Normally, Mark works three to eleven, but he called earlier, said he was sick again. He's a real sweetheart, Mark, but he's been having all sorts of health problems."

"I'll stay," I said. "Why don't you go ahead and go. Get some rest."

She paused a moment. Said, "No. I couldn't leave you alone so soon."

"I can handle it. I'll call you if I have any problems."

"I couldn't do that to you, Leo."

"I can handle it."

She paused again. "Are you sure?"

"I'm sure. Go rest."

Paused. "Might not be a bad idea. I been feeling plumb awful here lately."

"Go rest. Feel better."

"I can see I'm gonna like working with you, Leo." She pulled her purse out from under the counter, set it on her stool, and shuffled through it several seconds before pulling out a gargantuan set of keys. "Normally," she said, "they's a few things you're supposed to do on the nightshift, but since it's your first night and all, you can just sort of get broke in nice and slow. Normally, you're supposed to measure the gas and get the gas readings and clean out the bathrooms, and bag up some ice. My number's right here by the phone, case you need anything. I'll be home resting. You sure you going to be okay until six-thirty?"

"I'll be okay."

"I feel bad leaving you alone so soon."

"I'm a natural at this. It's my calling."

"I'll see you tomorrow morning then. My number's there on the counter."

"Okay then."

She filled a jumbo fountain Coke, took it out with her, and loaded her things slowly into her Ford LTD, white with red vinyl top, three missing hubcaps and a dented fender. She pulled away, waving over her shoulder, and I stood at the window waving back, already calculating that some thirteen and a half hours would pass before I could see her again.

24

Not a minute elapsed when someone wasn't in the store or pumping gas, and this made me doubt whether this job would work out after all. They bought milk and bread and beer and cigarettes. They bought packs of hotdogs and buns, and big bags of potato chips. They bought ice cream and candy bars and packs of sugar doughnuts. They bought two dollars worth of gas. They bought aspirin, NoDoz, and diet pills, and washed them down with Big Gulp fountain drinks. They came through as they got off work, avoiding all the people filling buggies in the cheaper supermarkets. They left their kids in the car, yelled at them to stay there, and came in, pulling wrinkled bills from dirty jeans. They came until it started getting dark. Then gaps of silence grew and I began to believe the job might work out after all.

I spent a religious half-hour with no sound at all except for the humming of the cooler motors. I stared through the window and entertained thoughts of sitting.

A procession of men in hard hats stopped on their way to the mill's graveyard. They stumbled to the back of the store and filled thermoses with coffee, walking like zombies, digging fingers into their eyes to chip away welded sleep. They stocked up on cigarettes and aspirin, chewing tobacco and candy bars. They bought beer and bags of ice to put in the coolers they kept in their truck beds until morning when they'd reach into them again. They bought microwave sandwiches and ate them leaning against the counter, saying little to one another, as if they'd all lived in the same house and knew better than to impress each other with being cheerful. They said things like, "Let's go make eight," and "Six on and three off." I made change for them and they thanked me, saying little else, which I didn't mind.

Those getting off second shift stopped in for the same things their coworkers had stopped for earlier, faces drenched in the same fatigue, though theirs came from craving sleep instead of trying to rise up out of it.

I got to know them by the things they bought. The big man who gulped three Yoohoos. The skinny kid who popped Tums like M&M's. The spicy-sausage eating man who sang bits of gospel hymns. The old man who turned up packs of Goody's to mute the machinery he said was locked inside his brain. The Goody's man emptied the pack on his tongue, needing nothing to wash it down, and then he winked and tossed the empty packet on the counter. I nodded respectfully, and threw it away, neither of us needing to say a word.

The silence came and promised to remain. I turned the thermostat to sixty, made fresh coffee and furnished the area behind the counter, where I hoped to remain unmoved till early morning. I moved the five-gallon bucket and the chair and aligned them so my feet would reach the former from the latter. I placed the chair flush against the rear counter, lowered myself into it, and raised my feet to the upturned bucket, happy with the slight degree of downward slope, which meant the circulation to my feet wouldn't be restricted. The chair looked as if it once belonged in someone's antique kitchen—metal legs and a red nylon cushion coming unstitched around the corners. Its legs were short enough so that my eyes were even with the underside of the counter in front of me. I couldn't see, or be seen, by anyone who might be standing on the other side, demanding things. Then I reached out and pulled Gladys's stool close enough to me that I could prop my left forearm on top of it and dangle my hand over the side, palming the top of my Styrofoam coffee cup. I could raise the cup and lower it again by moving only half an arm. Sometime later, I would come across a piece of reading on ergonomics, the science of efficient movement, and I'd feel a quiet rush of euphoria for not having had to read about it in the first place.

I sat in silence, sipping coffee. The night was silhouetted from the dim lights of the parking lot. I stared for hours into the night, losing time, letting my coffee go cold even as I held it in my hand. I let the silence wash over me, and stared out at the darkness. Felt something thawing in my mind. Started to see better inside the night. Started to see all the truth that was hidden by the sun. There is no truth beneath the sun. There is no sun above the truth. I could see because I wasn't moving. Inside the sun, among the ambitious voices racing to increase production, everything is moving and we cannot see. Inside the sun, we go blind. In the darkness there was nothing but the darkness to focus on, and the dark nothingness was beautiful. The silence adopted me. I knew the night would soon start asking questions the sun had hidden, and I grew excited. It would remind me that the sun hides the fact that there are no answers. I stared into the darkness until my eyes carved tunnels through it. Inside the silent tunnels of the night is where I lived. Inside these tunnels, I expected people to come and visit me—people who would help me organize my past and bury it. I saw a woman in North Carolina I'd almost married wiping the ass of a man who couldn't speak, and I wished her well. I saw the serene eyes of the invalid who had taken my place, and I also wished him well. I heard the screams of Dotty Kirkland, the third grader who drowned in a pond behind her school. I looked through the tunnels of the night until the blackness blurred and then I blinked and refocused on the blackness.

What the sun hides is history. The sun shines on the clock above city hall and teaches us to forget the stories of the defeated. But in the stillness of the night, I grew attuned to the battle cry of every misplaced ghost. I heard the stamping of the Cherokee, who dance on blistered feet. I heard the wails of the Miccusokee, and Chief Osceola, imprisoned for attending a peace talk scheduled beneath the sun. The sun hides the hungry and the homeless. It gets in the eyes and makes you believe everyone has what they deserve. The sun hides the hog shit in your cup of tea.

I blinked away the blurring blackness and refocused on the blackness, and there found a living figure staring back at me. A man standing on the elevated island of the gas pumps, leaning on one of them, elbow propped on top. He wore a misshapen red cap with a faded logo, dirty jeans and a torn T-shirt. He raised his left bicep to his mouth and bit it. He moved his mouth up and down his arm, biting his wrist and his forearm and the inset of his elbow, eyes constantly locked with mine. Then he lunged off the island and started toward the door in quick small steps, swinging his left arm wildly to the side, moving his lips in full conversation. I looked beneath the counter for a weapon, and spied a hammer, though the thought of using it forced me back to stillness. The man entered the store and stood before the counter while still holding to the door. I stood unsurely and gave him my most unthreatening nod. His pale blue eyes were glazed and dilated, and they moved rapidly in tiny semi-circles while he read the surface of my face.

"Got a cigarette?" he said.

"No," I said too quickly.

"Damn." He looked as if I'd hurt his feelings. He turned quickly, hung his head and started back through the door.

"Hold on," I said. I looked beneath the counter and removed a carton of generics I'd seen earlier—the carton used to replenish the stack of specials on sale for a dollar. I pulled out a pack from the carton and tossed them on the counter.

"I just need one," he said.

"Somebody left these. You can have them."

The man turned loose the door and stepped forward, grabbed the pack quickly and stuffed them in his pocket without looking at me.

"You need some matches?" I said.

He nodded, and I tossed a pack on the counter. He scooped them up, shoved them in his other pocket and then patted both pockets to make sure everything was in its rightful place. He paused a moment then, appearing to scan tabloid headlines.

He said, "I tell you I had heart surgery?"

"No, you didn't tell me that," I said.

"Still hurts like a motherfucker."

I played along. "Was it a quadruple bypass?"

"Yeah."

He continued scanning headlines, and I saw that he was harmless, that he was mostly afraid and untrusting, and that he might have his reasons.

"I had heart surgery once," I said. "This woman ripped it out and stomped all over it and sliced it up with a butcher knife and then crammed it back down my throat." I laughed, and surprised myself by laughing, but the man simply shook his head.

"They's some messed up people out there," he said.

"Yes," I said. "Yes there are."

He lifted his head from the tabloids and looked at me.

"Are you washed in the blood of the lamb?"

"What's that?"

"Have you been washed in the soul-cleansing blood of the lamb?"

I repeated a joke I'd heard a millworker tell another millworker who invited him to church: "Last time I went to church, the preacher tried to drown me."

He closed his eyes violently against the image of a murdering clergyman. He looked at the ground, said, "I feel like traveling on."

And then the man walked out, striding quickly across the dark parking lot, swinging his left arm way out to the side, and bringing up his right hand occasionally to pinch his nose. I watched him fade away into the darkness and then I watched the spot where he'd faded from, feeling lonely. I watched the spot until it carved a tunnel through the night, and then I stared through the tunnel for a while.

What the sun hides are those paid by the hour, delivering services for the salaried. It hides the frozen veins inside the ankles of the women who stand all day in ice and de-vein shrimp in the back room of private seafood plants. It hides the underside of the tables where folded bills are passed per pound. The sun hides the frozen bones the women take home and can't thaw out, even when they plant their feet inside five-gallon buckets of heated water. The sun hides the ethnic driver who delivers the tonnage of de-veined shrimp to the back doors of restaurants for the line of ethnic workers who will prep and sauté and cook and present them to the sunburned tourists so hungry for the blessings of fresh food. I stared into a tunnel of the night until a pair of headlights came driving out. A man in dirty clothes stepped out of it, reached over the tailgate as he rounded the truck, and pulled out what I thought might be a shotgun. He stepped through the door and I saw that what he was carrying was a fishing pole. He nodded politely and set the pole down across the counter.

"Let me ask you something," he said. He spread his hands on both sides of his pole, and leaned into the counter, eyes pointed toward his shoes.

I stayed seated.

He raised his head, slowly, and I saw in his eyes that the question he wanted to ask had been there forever without forming.

"This is a good fishing pole," he said. "Cost me eighty dollars three years ago. A Zebco 855 with thirty-pound test. I gave my kids all the food I had, and I've gone hungry three days now. My wife died last year, and I'm all out of bait and I can't catch a fucking thing no ways. I guess I ain't the fisherman I used to be. I used to could catch them all night long—Mullet." He dropped his head between his arms and quickly lifted it again.

"Let me trade you this pole for some groceries." His red eyes turned a shade softer, and for a moment he looked like a troubled child.

I stood unsurely, heels backed against my chair.

"It's a good pole," he said. "Cost me eighty dollars three years ago."

"Looks like a good pole," I said. "But we don't even sell them here or anything."

"Hadn't you got any use for it? How about ten dollars? Cost me eighty."

"Why don't you just keep your pole," I said, "and take this bag and fill it up with groceries and we'll call it even." I passed him a paper bag and looked out the window to see if any do-good cops were watching this self-inflicted robbery.

"You serious?"

"Just make it quick," I said.

"You sure you don't need a pole?"

I told him I was sure and repeated my plea for him to hurry.

The man took his bag up and down three aisles, raked in cans of Beanie-weenies, Vienna sausage, soups, Spam, beef jerky, bread and ketchup. He went to the cooler and brought out packs of bologna and premade sandwiches. Then he turned and muttered something that I didn't understand.

"Said you mind if I snag me a beer or two?"

"Help yourself."

He carried his bag to the counter, grabbed his fishing pole and stopped in front of the doors, his eyes welling with water.

"My name's Tommy Spencer," he said. "What's yours."

I told him.

"If I can ever do anything for you, I'll do it."

I said I'd let him know. He looked at me one last time and went out, put his groceries and fishing pole in the back of his truck and drove away.

I poured myself a fresh cup of coffee and settled back into my chair, feet propped on my upturned bucket. I sat there and looked through the window into the night and didn't move, except occasionally to raise my coffee cup.

What the sun hides is the availability of stillness. It hides the moment, which is forever concealed with planning ways to avoid regret. The sun hides the lie that movement alone produces greatness. The sun hides the holes inside the heads of teachers. It hides the space between backyard satellites and satellites parked in space. Which is the sky. What the sun hides is the *sky*.

It hides the telephone lines that travel between the mouths of reporters and the mouths of the administrators the reporters quote too carefully. The sun hides the fatigue that comes from being in the sun. The feeling of fatigue so strong that you can taste the crumbling dirt of your drying soul. It hides the madness that lives beneath the fatigue, when you feel yourself outside of your body, unable to recognize your mother.

I stared through a tunnel in the night until the blackness blurred, and then I blinked and watched Death walk through the tunnel and into the store, where he poured himself a cup of coffee. He dumped in creamer from a can, tore three packs of sugar one at the time and methodically stirred it all together with a wooden swizzle stick, thinking of other things. He had a full beard left untrimmed for months, and in his eyes there lived a wild animal that hadn't slept in twenty years. There was something strangely calming about him, however, which suggested that he had seen every form of evil and could no longer be surprised at anything.

I sipped my coffee and watched him sip his while he meandered slowly down the aisles, staring at merchandise as if it belonged in a museum. He came down the last aisle and stopped in front of the doors, staring out into the night. He sipped his coffee, and I sipped mine.

"It's quiet out there," he whispered.

"What's that?" I said.

"Quiet," he said louder. "It is *quiet*. Out *there*." He stared through the door.

I nodded. "It's slow alright."

The man laughed, moving his head but not his mouth. He stared, unblinking, into the night. He seemed to be staring across the street toward the motel.

"That smell," he said.

I nodded.

He said, "It seems especially bad on wet days and in the early mornings."

"It grows on you," I said.

He gave this a laugh that died as soon as it hit his lips.

Knowing nothing else to say, I asked him how his night was going.

He slowly repeated this, making a question of my question's relevance, stretching each word as if it were the first time he'd ever heard it. He lit a cigarette and sipped his coffee and stared out into the night.

"You want to know how my night's going?" he said.

Then I started feeling stupid. "If you feel like it, you know. Doesn't matter."

He took a toke from his cigarette and started speaking while smoke leaked slowly from his nose and mouth.

"My wife and I stopped here on a trip from Miami. We were going to visit her parents in Boston, to ask for money—again. My engine blew up less than a mile from here. She's a registered nurse and can't get work at the hospital because they use out-of-state temps. I pose as a security guard for that run-down deserted motel across the street where I make forty dollars a night, thirty of which I have to give back to my boss for the privilege of keeping our luxurious room with its roaches and tepid water. My father is dying in Ohio, but he and the rest of the family have refused to see me since 1965, when I went to Canada instead of Vietnam. My first wife has taken my sons to California and has gone to a judge who promptly classified me as a dead-beat dad. Last year at this time, I was a professor at a major university where I was denied tenure because I taught Mark Twain. It took me six years to earn a Ph.D.—for which I currently owe $20,000—and all I've put in my stomach so far today has been a bag of stale potato chips and this very wonderful cup of coffee. That's roughly how it's going." He lifted his cigarette, and chased it with a sip of coffee.

I asked him where he had taught.

"That's an insignificant detail," he said. "They all have the same name."

I nodded.

"Let me ask you something," the man said, addressing the window.

"Okay."

"How would you feel about giving me a line of credit?" He turned from the door then and looked at me for the first time. His eyes were dark and cold and red.

"Okay," I said, but he hadn't heard.

"I know that kind of thing's not done much any more, but this would be strictly between you and me. Let me fill up a couple of bags of groceries, tally up what I owe you, and I'll make payments on it every day."

"Sure," I said.

"My wife will have a job sometime soon, probably. And it's not like we'll be going anywhere."

"Okay," I said.

"We'll be right across the street, and you'll see me every night."

"Right," I said. "Okay."

The man fell silent then. He looked me in the eyes and nodded once with appreciation. I handed him two bags, and he took them one at the time up and down three aisles, riddled with tough choices. He pulled off cans, read the back of them and put them back. He went to the cooler and pulled out sandwich meat and a pack of cheese. He dropped cookies and doughnuts into the tops of his bags and moved his eyes over items behind the counter.

"How you fixed for smokes?" I said.

He almost smiled. "Pack of Camels for me and a pack of Salem's for the wife."

I pulled down two packs and tossed them in a bag, and pushed the bag closer to him. He looked deeply into my eyes, seeming to say thank you.

"You got it all totaled up?" he said.

"I got it."

"You add the cigarettes?"

"I added them."

He picked up the bags and walked backwards out the door, staring at me deeply, saying nothing. His eyes were full of pity and gratitude and the promise of sleeping on a full stomach. His eyes seemed to anticipate his wife's eyes when she'd look up from the television through clouds of cigarette smoke and see him holding two full bags of groceries. I watched him walk across the parking lot and disappear behind a motel door, and then I stared for a while into the darkness.

I stared at the darkness and thought of my life many years from now, when I might still be staring at the darkness, feet propped on an upturned bucket. And I thought of myself many years after that, sitting in this same spot at the age of seventy, wise from watching people come and go, but broke and still alone. I wondered if the silence might grow too large. I wondered if it would swallow me and make me miss the sun. I wondered if I would ever touch, or be touched again by a woman. Imagined it a death like starving. I saw through a tunnel in the night, myself, aching with the yearnings of old men. The sun hides the desperation in the perimeter of the pupil. Desperation lives in the heart of the heart of the night, next to regret and fear. The sun hides the loneliness that thrives inside the night. The depth of loneliness that breeds the fear of death.

25

Stared at the night until the sky cracked with specks of light as big as fingernails. Gladys came in and caught me staring. She came in with half-closed eyes, carrying a long-stemmed rose inside a Styrofoam cup. She put her rose on the counter and mumbled morning greetings. She grabbed a bag of peanuts, went to the cooler for a Coke and came behind the counter, where she proceeded to pour the peanuts into the Coke.

"Lord-God have mercy," she said. "I feel awful this morning, Leo. They's some mornings I just think I could sleep forever. You know what I mean?"

"I know what you mean," I said. "I really do."

She drank her Coke.

"Look what I growed," she said, and nodded toward her rose.

"That's nice," I said.

"I got me a little rose garden outside my trailer I been pruning on of the evening. Smell of it." She pushed the cup toward me.

"That's nice."

"I got red ones too. I'll bring you one tomorrow you can give your sweetheart. You got a sweetheart?"

"No. Nobody serious, you know."

"I ain't neither. I ain't had no nookie in I don't know how long. I stay so busy working and looking after my boy and my mama and my roses till there ain't hardly time to rest, let alone be a-courting somebody."

"I know what you mean," I said.

"My boy, especially, needs lots of attention. He got into gas when he was real little, but I don't know whether or not that's got anything to do with it. I just know he acts a little hopeless, you know. You can see it in a young'uns face when they seem hopeless." She drank from her Coke again, chewed her peanuts, and leaned against the counter next to the spot where I was leaning. Our shoulders touched.

"Got into gas?" I said.

"He fell into a bucket of gas when he was eighteen months old and liked to drowned."

"My goodness."

"It was his daddy's fault. His daddy wadn't watching him like he was supposed to be. He had this bucket of gas sitting out—using it to kill off all the fire ants around the house—and my boy, he just went right over to it and stuck his head all the way down in it." She shook her head, and stared through the window at a single spot of history.

"I'm real sorry to hear that," I said. And I was. I was even surprised at my earnest tone.

She laughed. She looked me in the eye and I felt a chill. "It's just one more thing you have to worry over in this life is all. Let's get you rung out so you can get on home. I imagine you're about tired, ain't you?"

"Not really," I said. "It was real slow."

"It always is on the graveyard. But they insist on staying open on account of we're the only store around here. She took a big gulp from her Coke, set it on the counter, and stepped toward the register, as if it were a monumental task she'd been gearing up for.

"All you got to do," she said, "is turn this key over here to Z like this and then hit the cash button. And then take out your money and count it, and subtract a hundred and fifty, which is what you started out with, and see if it matches up with the tape. You can go ahead and count your drawer, if you want to."

I counted my drawer, drawing it out so I could spend more time with Gladys. I added amounts from the columns of gas and grocery and beer and cigarettes and candy and misc. and then added the columns together and subtracted one-fifty. Then I did it again because the final figure didn't match the tape.

"I'm fifty-seven dollars and sixteen cents short," I said.

"It was your first night. Might take a while to get the hang of it. Go home and get some rest."

I didn't really want to leave, but she seemed ready to begin her morning duties, so I walked around the counter and toward the door.

"Luke'll be working tonight when you come in," she said. "He's the regular three to eleven guy. He was supposed to work yesterday, but he called in sick.

He's been sick a lot lately." She shrugged and straightened a stack of papers.

"I'll see you tomorrow then," I said, and, waving, stepped through the door.

She lit a cigarette and waved back.

I walked home beneath the breaking light, feeling good about being at the end of the right end of the day. There was no traffic. The surfaces of houses were coated in shadows and soft light. And only a few birds were squawking, as if to report the news that the night had been a lie.

I went straight for my metal rocking chair and sat beneath the rising sun, feeling strangely lucid. The sky was the color of a fading bruise. The air was soft and perfect. Birds took turns, subtly singing chorus. I rocked in my metal rocking chair and vowed never to sleep again. I rocked until the sun stole every pocket of the sky and then I stuck my head inside E.B.'s door and yelled for him to cook some breakfast for a working man. His house was bare—no rugs to hide the plywood floors, no flowered wallpaper to hide the dirty sheetrock, no curtains to hide the sun.

"Stop sleeping your life away," I yelled.

I walked down the hall, the exact width of mother's hall, and then entered a bedroom the exact dimensions of mother's room.

"Day's half gone," I said.

I sank into the wheelchair beside his bed and stared at his body, already knowing he was dead. A quilt was tucked neatly beneath his chin, and his face was facing mine, mouth gaped open, two lonely teeth exposed like sagging fence posts. Without his glasses, his face looked as if it had collapsed in the night. Mounds of wrinkles merged with a caved forehead, burying his eyes. Deep wrinkles like pictures of dried up rivers. I sat in his wheelchair and didn't move. The silence hatched in my stomach and germinated. On the other side of his bed was a wooden chair with a pot hanging in a hole, roll of toilet paper on the arm. A party of flies danced above the pot. Piles of shoes lay scattered in the farthest corner. The room smelled of dust and cooked tobacco. A dirty sheet was nailed over the only window. I sat in his wheelchair and didn't move. I didn't know the proper thing to do. I wondered then if I knew anyone who knew the proper thing to do, and I thought of mother. But I didn't want to bother her in case she might be sleeping, and so I tried to think of someone else who knew the proper thing to do, but there was no one. I watched a fly rub its hind legs after perching on my hand. A picture of a phone came to me and I wondered how long it would take to picture the proper person to call. I thought of the police, but that was wrong, and then the hospital, also wrong, and then I thought of calling my old newspaper to recite an obituary, but that was also wrong. Then I thought of the funeral home I passed on my way to work, and knew that would be a good place to start. I watched two flies fucking on my hand. E. B. didn't own a phone.

I got out of his wheelchair and walked down his hall and went next door and fingered the yellow pages for the right place to call, and then I called. Then I went down the hall to tell mother, but she was sleeping—breath coming out like cracked whistles—so I left her and went back to the loveseat where I tried to sleep while they came and got the body. But I couldn't sleep because the sun was bleeding too brightly into the room and all I could see was the shrunken face of E.B. Miller, who spent the end of his life telling stories to people who did not listen.

I didn't move until much later, when I saw mother coming down the tunnel of the hall, slippers sliding, and then I moved my head to face her face, and said, "E.B.'s dead."

She fell back against the kitchen doorway. Her face was impossibly blank, though there was a face beneath her face that was clearly breaking.

"That's no way to break news like that," she said. "No way at all."

In the silence that fell between us then, I realized she must be right. I tried to think of a better way I could've broken news like that. I should have told her to sit down and warned her I had bad news so she could start preparing the face beneath the face that might start breaking. But it was too late. The beans had spilled, and the face beneath the face had broken, and a landmark had been erected in the silence to forever mark this moment when I broke the news the way I broke it. She stayed propped against the wall, staring at the landmark.

"Did you call anyone?"

I nodded, but the nod wasn't loud enough and so she had to repeat herself. I looked at her, clearly at her then, and nodded clearly—a distinct and clear-cut nod.

"Your attitude stinks," she said.

She turned and went back down the tunnel of the hall, slippers sliding.

I fell back on the loveseat and didn't sleep. I stared at the ceiling for several hours, then I went to work without having slept at all. I went to work two hours early, at nine p.m., to look out a different window. I walked to the store and met Mark, a large black man who sat on the stool behind the counter, painting his fingernails. He didn't look up when I walked in. I went to the back, filled a coffee cup and brought it back behind the counter.

"I'm Leo," I said. "New guy."

Mark turned on the stool and looked over the top of his square-framed glasses.

"Why are you *here?*" He looked at his watch.

"I just felt like coming in. You want me to go ahead and clock in? I don't mind."

He curled up one side of his mouth. "Are you serious?"

"Sure," I said.

"Just let me finish up these last two fingers."

I watched Mark's fat fingers work the dainty brush across the last two nails on his left hand. I couldn't tell any difference though between the colors of the painted nails and those he was painting now. And I felt like asking. I felt like being friends with Mark. I imagined it was difficult for him to live in a town like this. I wanted to hear his stories of surviving loneliness.

"Why do you use clear paint?"

"Prevents chipping," he said.

I wanted to get him talking. But I didn't know where to start. And before I could think of a starting place, he had walked around me and out the door, offering a cold, "See 'ya" over the shoulder.

I arranged my furniture. Brought up my chair and upturned bucket, and placed the stool as an armrest to my left. I sat in the silence and stared through the window at the night. I stared at the darkness without interruption. I stared through the window at the darkness. I could see everything. The street was bare. The motel was completely empty. The Shipwreck Lounge was dead. I sat and watched the still world, and I could see very clearly even the smallest things. The head of a bulldog was painted on the door of the Shipwreck Lounge. The bulldog wore a red collar and black spikes. There were six whiskers on each side of the bulldog's mouth, and two bottom teeth rising to sharp points. There was a single speck of white inside the oval of his muddy eyes. Dark lines were cast in the flesh beneath his eyes. Folds in the hanging jowls.

I gave mill workers coffee and Yahoo's and Goody's headache powders.

Johnny came in at two, and I gave him cigarettes.

"Are you washed in the blood?" he said.

"Sure."

"I got a home in Beulah land," he said.

I gave him matches.

"I'm headed to God's celestial shore," he said. "I feel like traveling on." And then he left, walking quickly through the parking lot, raising his left arm wildly out to the side, raising his right hand to pinch his nose.

What the sun hides are the owners of the oceans. It hides their ancestors, a group of New York bankers who didn't come to Jekyll Island in 1910 for private hunting. What the sun hides is the dreamless sleep of the bosses who never have to see their workers. It hides the deep rest bosses get on expensive mattresses inside well-insulated houses. It hides the goose down pillows that cradle their rich heads. The sun hides the schemes concocted by the elected who spend their nights planning spins for morning cameras. It hides the cobwebs on the combination locks stored in banker's basements.

I looked over a list of numbers taped to the register, and entertained thoughts of calling Gladys, just to chat, to say everything was fine and that I was enjoying myself, but I knew she'd be asleep and that she was clinging fiercely to every minute she could steal. Beneath her number was a number for Clarence Love, owner of this store and many like it. Lived in Savannah. I'd heard his name slurred from the mouth of Gladys, full of derision for having refused her raises for five years.

The phone rang five times before he picked up and mumbled incoherently.

"Is this Clarence Love?"

"Who wants to know?"

"My name's Leo Gray. I work for you."

"What the hell time is it?"

I looked at the register clock. "It is the hell of two a.m., sir."

"What do you want?"

"I'll need a raise, sir."

Seconds of silence. "Call my office tomorrow," he said, and then hung up.

I called right back, said, "we seem to have been disconnected."

"What's your name again?"

"Leo Gray. I work for you at Texaco 166, in Milton."

"It's two a.m." he said.

"You're currently paying me $5.50 an hour. I think I deserve at least $5.75. I have bills."

"Look, my son will be around there in the next few days and he'll talk to Gladys about your performance and we'll take it into consideration."

"Take it into consideration? That's not much of an answer."

Clarence Love sighed.

"I have a kid and wives," I said.

Clarence Love hung up.

I called right back. Busy.

I looked through the window for awhile, picturing Clarence Love already having fallen into sleep, mixing his dreams with strange calls he'd forget when he later settled into breakfast and the morning newspaper.

What the sun hides is the regret that hides inside the smiles that shine inside the day. At night, if the night is truly dark and truly quiet, regret is seen for what it is, which is the stupidity of desire.

The motel man came in at four, poured himself a cup of coffee and wandered up and down the aisles until he got to the front door again, where he stopped and stared into the night.

"My wife said to thank you," he said.

I sipped coffee and nodded.

"She's sick. Bronchitis, I think."

"I'm sorry to hear that," I said.

He shrugged, sipped coffee, and stared unblinking toward his motel.

"She thinks it's the air here, but it could be the air anywhere."

I nodded.

"Baudelaire said, 'Life is a hospital," he said. "'Where every patient is obsessed with changing beds. Some think they'll suffer less by the stove and others think they'll get better by the window.'"

I thought I should understand, but I didn't, and so I nodded.

He gulped the last of his coffee and dropped his cup into the trashcan.

"Are you aware of the moment when civilization ended?" he said.

"The moment?"

"According to Rousseau, civilization ended in the exact moment when the first man built the first moat, thereby making claims to property. That's when civilization ended."

I thought I should understand again, but I didn't, and so I nodded.

"Put the coffee on my bill," he said.

"Got it," I said.

"See you tomorrow."

I nodded again, and looked out the window. I stared out into the night until the night grew pale, and then I began my routine of jobs. I filled fifty bags of ice and stacked them neatly. Measured the gas wells with a forty-foot wooden pole. Took a clipboard to the gas tanks and wrote down the string of tiny black numbers beneath the larger numbers. Swept and mopped the entire store, and two bathrooms. Emptied trashcans into the dumpster and relined the cans, tying neat knots. Stood for awhile beside the dumpster and looked into the night at the scattered stars, refusing to see constellations.

Gladys pulled into the parking lot and caught me staring. She muttered morning greetings and shuffled inside, straight for her sixteen ounce Coke and bag of peanuts. I followed her, truly glad to see her. I went behind the counter and removed my furniture and placed the stool where I thought she'd like it. I wanted to know how she was doing.

She plopped onto the stool and sighed.

"God have mercy," she said.

I leaned on the counter next to her and asked her what was wrong.

"I blew up my kitchen last night," she said. "I was frying some catfish and before I knew it I had me an out of control fire going on. Mama—she started screaming for me to call 911, and then me and her and my son run outside and before I knew it all these volunteer firemen started racing up in their trucks and pretty soon after that a big 'ol fire engine. I was scared to death something was going to blow up, but this one fireman he told me, he said, that only happens in the movies. But Lord have mercy—my cabinets. All my cabinets and part of my ceiling's burnt. I'm lucky the whole place didn't go up. And us with no insurance."

"Do you have a fire extinguisher?"

"You know, that's the same thing that fireman asked. I told *him*, I said, 'I sure don't, but I'm going to run out and get me one.' It just never has dawned on me to get one. I guess it's one a them things you don't think about it till it's too late, you know?'

"I know," I said. "I know."

"Course my catfish was rurnt. I never did get no supper."

"I'm sorry," I said.

She sighed, gulped the last of her Coke and lit a cigarette. "You want to work for me a couple hours this afternoon, say from about noon to three, so I can run out to Wal-Mart and get me a fire extinguisher and see about some new cabinets?"

"I could do that," I said. "I'd be glad to."

"I sure appreciate it. Mark will be here at three. If you could come in about noon I could go and get my shopping done before it gets so crowded in there you can't hardly move. And it's just about impossible to get waited on. I almost had me a panic attack last time I was in there. It's a like a zoo. You wouldn't believe some of the people in there—the way they dress and all—like they don't have a bit of pride. I swear to God it looks like some of them crawled out of the swamp. You need me to pick you up anything?"

"No," I said. "I don't guess I need anything." I looked out the window at the breaking light.

"What's the matter?" she said.

"My uncle. Well, not really my uncle, but my neighbor who was like my uncle—he died yesterday. I think it was yesterday. I lose track of the days."

"Gosh, Leo. I'm sorry. That's awful."

I nodded and looked out the window.

"How about a hug?" She got off her stool and came toward me then, arms stretched wide.

I stepped into them. She squeezed me firmly and didn't pat my back. She held me tightly, with all her girth and strength, and it felt good. I rested my head against her shoulder and closed my eyes. She had the biggest heart I'd ever put my ear against, and I wanted to listen to it until it cajoled me into sleep.

"Sometime after I get my kitchen fixed I want you to come over so I can cook you some supper."

I nodded against her shoulder.

"We'll lock Mama in her room."

I nodded again.

She patted my back and stepped away.

"You'd better go on home and get you some sleep," she said.

I nodded.

"You try to stay strong," she said.

I nodded and walked out into the morning. I walked home through the dim light breaking open on the world. It was the first sunrise I thought I'd ever *felt* while walking, when the rhythm of my steps matched the rhythm of its unfolding. I couldn't yet see the sun. All I could see was a smear of purple wrapped in a streak of orange, and it was like an all-knowing giant bulb whose dimmer switch was at its dimmest. The red bricks of the housing projects glowed metallic. I wanted to knock on all the doors of the shotgun shacks I passed so the people could come and witness the spectacle of the rising sun. Walked through my yard and sank into my metal rocking chair. Listened to several birds whose names I didn't care about. Watched the day break open and vowed never to sleep again.

Sat with locked hands, still as a statue. Didn't twiddle my thumbs and didn't tap my feet and didn't move my head from side to side so my eyes could work. Sat and stared at whatever crossed my line of vision. Saw misshapen animals blurring past in speeding cars. The ringing rose up in my ear and tapped bright circles in the basement of my brain. I knew mother was there behind me, leaning against the screen, because I heard her breathing. I knew she was there, but I didn't let her know I knew until she coughed her throat-clearing cough that started an avalanche of coughing. Then I turned and said good morning. She was in bathrobe and slippers, one side of her hair matted down from sleeping.

"Service is this morning at ten," she said. "They didn't see any need to wait since nobody's coming in from out of town or anything. I guess we'll be the only ones there."

"Okay," I said.

"Don't you want to take a nap?"

I shook my head.

"It's just going to be a little graveside service. They already have the body there. I talked to them on the phone. I told him we didn't have a way to get there, and they said they'd send a car for us. I'm not really up to going to any funerals. But I guess we don't have much choice."

I nodded.

She waited a few seconds and went inside.

I stayed in my metal rocking chair, unmoving. I closed my eyes but didn't sleep. The sun grew harsh and the cars came fast. Tractor-trailers raced with full beds toward the mill and raced with empty beds away. I was tired and disoriented from being sleepless, but it felt good. My eyes narrowed into camera lenses and found small things to focus on. I saw the distinct shape of each piece of bark attached to the trees stacked in moving trailers. Each piece connected to a pattern resembling the skin of certain snakes. I saw the hair on the arms of drivers; saw their knotted elbows perched on top of windows. Sat still until a black Cadillac pulled up.

Mother came out in her tight red dress and we got into the back seat of the Cadillac. She looked out of her window and I looked out of mine, neither of us speaking to the young driver who wore his black cap crooked, and drank from a sacked bottle he claimed was juice. We passed tiny houses with dirt yards, stopping at stop signs on every block. We passed rotting wooden fences wrapped in Christmas lights; caved roofs holding satellite dishes; a lady in a bathrobe watering brown plants. Passed a purple duplex and a pink duplex, and then a squat wooden home knocked loose from its foundation, windows shattered, vines growing through the porch, a no-smoking sign hung to a slanting porch post.

We were the only ones at the service except for a preacher neither of us had ever seen who kept us too long beneath the tent that was beneath the sun, talking of the valley of the shadow. Two cemetery workers in brown jumpsuits leaned on a tractor in the distance, smoking cigarettes. Then we shook hands with the preacher and went back home the way we came, thanking the young driver with the crooked hat who left the car in drive, stopping long enough for us to get out, before he sped away and cranked the bass of the car stereo, booming like a heartbeat.

I went straight to my metal rocking chair and mother went inside. I looked into a nearby tree; counted the veins on the bellies of the leaves. Saw my tailless squirrel in a low crook staring back at me while he rotated an acorn with four black claws attached to the end of four small fingers. Looked up from the squirrel into the sky, where a dozen buzzards glided gracefully, rising and dipping in currents of air I could almost feel. And then I walked to my job.

It was too hot for anyone to be outside. All the porches were vacant, and the road was empty, except for the occasional pine-hauling semi-trailer blowing waves of hot diesel into my face. Sweat dripped from me while I walked, but I didn't mind. I imagined each drop of sweat containing toxins that were divorcing me, gradually, like my psoriasis. I tried to think of what day it was, but I couldn't, and then I couldn't think of a single good reason why I should need to know.

Gladys smiled when I walked in, happy to see me. She gave a man his change, backed up a couple steps and unloaded her weight onto her stool, sighing deeply, reaching for her cigarettes.

"God have mercy," she said.

I asked her what was wrong.

"This is the first time I've sat down all morning. My mama keeps calling, complaining about her heart, and I had me a drive-off this morning worth fifteen dollars and some odd cents and between customers I been doing inventory, and either I can't add too good, or we're short by about a thousand dollars worth of stuff. But at least you're here now, so I can go ahead to the Wal-Mart and get my fire extinguisher. I sure appreciate you coming in like this. I'll make it up to you soon as I get my kitchen fixed. We'll have us a good supper one night soon."

"I'm looking forward to it," I said. And I was. I pictured us sitting at a small table in the kitchen of her trailer. Pictured me getting along with her son, who once got into gas. Pictured the three of us taking long walks, and holding hands.

"I'll be back by three, unless I get hit by a train or something."

"Take your time," I said.

"I sure appreciate it," she said. She gathered up her purse, stepped toward me, and kissed my cheek. "Why are you so nice to me?" she said.

"You're easy to be nice to," I said.

She shook her head, and walked away.

Customers came in waves over lunch hours, buying things to get them through the afternoon. They bought cigarettes and lottery tickets; big fountain drinks and single packs of aspirin. They bought bags of chips and glazed honey-buns.

I smiled at the faces facing me and asked how they were doing. Most said fine, or okay, but I held their eyes an extra beat to give them a second chance at the truth. A man wearing sunglasses bought a case of beer and said, "not worth a good goddamn. How *you* doing?"

I laughed, and told him honestly that I was doing fine.

"I'll be better after this is gone." He patted his beer and walked out.

A man in a suit bought Red Man, a Big Butt magazine and breath mints. A tired older man in a fast-food uniform bought a pack of rolling papers and Visine.

They bought Tylenol cold and flu medicine. They bought No-Doz and tabloid magazines. They bought diet pills and candy bars. Diet Pepsis and Honeybuns.

A man with the eyes of a Basset Hound stopped his van and filled a newspaper rack with *The Coastal Georgia Sun*. Then he came inside, went to the beer cooler and brought back a quart of Pabst Blue Ribbon.

I asked how he was doing.

He laughed the kind of laugh you hear in hospitals. Twisted his beer cap and took a hit. "Can I do this in here? Is that legal?"

"Sure," I said.

"My fourth one today," he said. "I've been drinking me a few of these every afternoon since a couple of weeks ago when I killed my little girl. Ran over her in that van right out there." He took another gulp. "She used to go with me on my route—sat in the open door there and tossed out papers. I went real slow and all, but one day I hit a bump and before I knew it I'd run over her with my back wheels. The doctor's had me on nerve pills, but they ain't helping a whole hell of a lot, you know? My wife says I been talking too much—been talking non-stop to anybody who'll listen for a half second, but that's the only thing seems to help, you know, more than the pills and this here. How much I owe you?"

I shook my head. "On the house," I said.

"I can't stop seeing it. In my mind, you know? Won't go away. Never will. It's just a job I took for extra money, you know, and I took her along 'cause it's the only time I had to be with her. What's your name?"

"Leo Gray," I said.

"I'm Johnny Boyd. My girl's name was Melissa. She was three. I don't know if I'm ever going to be all right again or not. I don't see how. Do you?"

I shook my head, half-smiling at the counter. There was nothing to say.

"Reckon I'll get back to it," he said. "Preciate the beer."

I nodded. "Anytime," I said.

The phone rang at 2:55. Mark said, "Where's Gladys?"

"Wal-Mart."

"I'm at the emergency clinic waiting to see a doctor for some antibiotics. Can you stay there another half-hour?"

"You want me to work your shift for you?"

"You don't have to be a smart-ass," Mark said. "I swear to God, I'm calling from the emergency clinic, where I've been for the past three hours, trying to get some fucking antibiotics."

"I'm serious," I said. "I'll work your shift for you."

He paused. "Are you crazy or something?"

"I don't mind. Really."

He paused again. "Okay. Tell Gladys I'll see her tomorrow."

"Hope you get to feeling better."

He hung up.

They bought half gallons of milk and whole gallons of ice cream and cases of Milwaukee's Best. They bought M&M's and lollipops and St. John's Wort. They bought generic cartons and packs of Nicoderm. Motor oil and a dollar's worth of gas. I got to where I could reach above my head for requested brands of cigarettes without looking. A barefooted woman holding a kid on her hip said she'd dropped a dollar bill while she was walking, and I told her not to worry about it.

Gladys came in sighing.

"God have mercy," she said.

I was counting pennies from a shirtless kid who bought a pack of Camels. The kid looked at the enormous woman who had just walked in, eyes widened in disbelief. Gladys walked around the counter and plopped down onto the stool.

"I had a nervous breakdown, Leo," she said.

The kid stared at her while he walked backwards out the door, banging the end of the pack against his palm.

"Just now?" I said.

"In 1977." She plucked a bag of M&M's from the display rack and tore them open with her teeth.

"It was right after I got divorced, and I was working two jobs down in

Miami 'cause I had a boy to feed, and I was going without sleep for about a week at the time. Then my boss at the Winn Dixie, he told me I'd either have to learn to speak Spanish or look for another job. We didn't have a pot to piss in. I don't remember much about what happened that summer, but my boy, Edward, he said I took two platefuls of spaghetti and flung 'em against the wall. Then he said I took all the dirty dishes that was sitting in the sink and threw them out the window. I finally went to the doctor and got calmed down, but he told me, he said if I wasn't careful that kind of thing could happen again at about anytime. Every morning when I come in here, I wonder if this'll be the day."

I nodded. "Should I take the Spaghettio-s off the shelf?"

"Sometimes, my heart. It'll just go to beating like crazy, and I'll think Lord-God have mercy, don't let me go now. When that happens, it's like I forget to breathe. That's what it feels like. Like I forget to breathe."

"I know what you mean," I said.

"You do?"

I nodded.

An ambulance blared past us then, siren shrieking loud enough to make me jump. I thought of mother—thought of sprinting home. Then Gladys said something that made me love her.

She said, "Reckon how many accidents is caused by the sound of sirens?"

We stared at each other.

She said, "That's sort of—what's the word?"

I crawled inside her pupils.

"I know what you mean," I said.

Her eyes started glistening.

"I bet you could use a hug," I said.

"I ain't had one since the last time."

She stood from her stool and I walked into her arms and let her squeeze. I let her squeeze until she finished squeezing.

A hollow-eyed man in wrinkled clothes walked in and went toward the coffee, and Gladys let go, giggling like a schoolgirl.

"I get worked up sometimes, I guess," she said.

"Me too," I said.

She sighed deeply and sat on her stool. She looked at her watch and jumped back up.

"Where's Mark?" she said.

"At the emergency clinic. He called."

"What's *his* problem?"

"He sounded real sick."

"God have mercy. Everything's just going to hell. If it ain't one thing it's two."

"I told him I'd work for him."

"No, Leo. I can't let you do that. You must be about to drop."

"I'm fine," I said. "I don't need much sleep these days."

The hollow-eyed man put his coffee on the counter and dropped a credit card next to it. I looked at him to see if he was serious.

"For the gas," he said.

I slid his credit card through the machine and asked how he was doing.

"I'm dead," he said. "That highway it beats you."

I nodded.

I pointed out the window. "There's an empty motel across the street."

"I've got to get to Jupiter, Florida. My brother called last night, said he was pissing blood."

I gave him back his card, looked him in the eye and said "good luck."

"Thanks for the coffee," he said, and quickly walked out the door.

Gladys said, "I don't know what we're going to do with Mark. He's always sick."

"Don't worry about it. I'll work his shift and mine too. Why don't you go on home and get some rest. Try out your new fire extinguisher."

"I'm going to fix us up a good supper one night soon. You bring the beer and we'll lock Mama in her room and have us a good time." She got off her stool and stood staring at me for a long moment.

"Yes we will," I said. "I'll bring the beer and we'll have a good time."

She patted my shoulder, picked up her purse and walked back around the counter and out the door, plucking two bags of M&M's on her way, jiggling her fingers at me through the window once she stepped outside.

They came through the afternoon, complaining of the heat and the need for rain. They bought quarts of Old Milwaukee and ice cream sandwiches. Popsicles and Hustler magazines. They stopped on their way from work, buying hot dogs and bologna and little jars of mustard. Microwave burritos with twelve packs of Hamm's. Rolling papers and bags of chips. Gas in increments as low as thirty-seven cents.

Dusk lingered for an hour, casting amber puddles, and my mind grew light. I watched every pocket of blue sky fade to black, and I quietly grew lucid. I turned the thermostat to sixty, sipped coffee from a Styrofoam cup and stared through my window at the darkening sky. Felt my memory thawing. I remembered part of a book, but not yet the author, about a man who met the Buddha in the woods and respectfully refused to follow him because he didn't believe wisdom could come from teachers.

The men coming off second shift at the mill needed the same things as the men going into third shift. I sometimes asked how they were doing. The man who guzzled three bottled Yoohoos said he felt like death warmed over. The man who poured Goody's powders on his tongue said never better. The man who ate spicy sausage and sang gospel hymns said the Lord was testing him.

When their eyes were too tired to notice, I gave them things. If they gave me a five-dollar bill, for example, I gave back four ones and four quarters. They thanked me with a nod or a wave and stepped blindly back into the night.

I arranged my furniture, sank into my chair and looked through my window. The only sound was the humming of the cooler motors. I sat, unmoving, and stared into the night.

What the sun hides is the moon and the man inside of it, who holds up a twenty-nine cent mirror. I stared into a tunnel of the night until a man on a bicycle came through it and then I stared at him. He leaned his bike on the ice machine and came inside. I couldn't see him from my low perch and he couldn't see me. He seemed to be standing just inside the door, looking for me. Waited to see what he would do. Waited to see if he would help himself to something and quickly leave so I wouldn't have to move. Gave him ample time. Gave him more than enough time.

"Hello?" he finally cried.

I didn't answer.

"Hello?" he said louder.

"Hello," I said, unmoving.

He stepped up to the counter then, looked over it and saw me sitting in my low chair. He was wearing an army jacket and sunglasses.

"You got it made back there," he said.

"Yes I do," I said.

He plopped a plastic bag on the counter, spilling videos.

"Five dollars each," he said.

"What are they?" I said.

"What are you into? I got women with men, women with women, men with kids, women with animals—not for everyone mind you—but high quality guaranteed."

"I see," I said. "Do you happen to be in any of these particular features?"

"I direct," he said. "Although I do have some cameos. What are you into?"

"I guess I'll pass. I don't even have a VCR or anything."

"I'll bring you one, thirty dollars guaranteed."

"Thanks, but I don't guess I'd be interested. I don't really have the time."

"I'm just trying to put some food on the table," he said. "I've got a wife and kids."

"Are they actors?"

The man didn't change expressions, and from this I sensed I had hurt his feelings. I saw my own face reflected back to me in his sunglasses and saw that I had been too cruel.

"There's no need to be insulting," he said. "As a matter of fact, they're not actors. They don't even know I'm out here in the dead of night, trying my best to keep them from going hungry. I'm trying my best to have a pleasant and pressure-free transaction and you have to go and condescend. Sorry I wasted your precious time." He gathered his bag of videos and stepped to the door, trailing a resentful stare.

"Hold up," I said, still seated.

He stepped to the counter again and stared, saying nothing.

"If they're not too picky," I said, "there's some refrigerated sandwiches over there I could let you, you know, let you have. Surplus inventory."

"I don't need your pity, Bub. I was doing just fine before I came in here and started getting insulted."

"The submarines aren't half bad. And there's ham and cheese."

"Anything on whole wheat?"

"Maybe."

He took his bag of videos to the cooler and filled it with sandwiches. He stopped in front of the counter on his way out and thanked me with a gentle bow instead of words.

Except for the humming of the cooler motors, the place was silent. I sat and stared through the tunnels of the night. The sun hides the secrets of those who prefer the underground. It hides the motivations behind piercings and tattoos—that the only thing owned by the dispossessed is the body, a fact which must be advertised. The sun hides the pale faces of kids who want to live inside computers. It hides the dark rooms where kids avoid the sun. What the sun hides is light itself.

Johnny came in at two, face covered in blood, though he didn't seem to know it. He stood flush against the counter, head framed in the small space between the register and a display rack of generic cigarettes.

"Got a cigarette?" he said.

I stood and tossed him a pack of generics, along with some matches. Waited for him to explain the blood. He packed his cigarettes calmly in his palm, unwrapped them and put one in his mouth, lighting it with a steady hand, volunteering nothing.

So I asked. Said, "What happened to your face there, buddy?"

He dropped his spent match on the floor, looked at me with squinted eyes through a wave of smoke and said, "I don't believe that's any of your fucking business, captain." He stared for a while with squinted eyes.

"How much is a beer?" he said.

"I can't sell beer after two a.m., Johnny." This was the first time I'd called him by his name, but he didn't seem surprised. He didn't ask how I knew his name, and he didn't ask for mine in return. His eyes dipped to the floor, seemingly saddened and betrayed. I wasn't afraid of selling past two a.m., but Gladys had told me that beer made Johnny dangerous because it interacted with whatever medicine he was on.

"Shit," he said. His voice turned soft, like a pleading child. "I won't tell nobody."

"See those cameras?" I said, pointing behind and above to two toy cameras hung as decoys by Clarence Love. "One of those cameras goes straight to the police station. There's some fat joker down there who sits behind a desk and watches to see if I sell a beer after two o'clock."

Johnny leaned his upper body over the counter and stared into a toy camera. "Joker," he yelled. Then he surprised me with a big belly laugh—surprised me with the condition of his cracked teeth, now caked with blood. He stopped suddenly, turned at me with a dour expression. The whites around his eyes shined next to the blood. His eyes dipped into the sadness and stared at me intently.

"Go get you a beer, Johnny."

He nodded in agreement, not smiling, as if he'd heard a good idea a long time in the making. He buried a beer can in each of his front jean pockets and stopped in front of the door.

"God's gonna send the water from Zion," he said.

"Yes," I said. "Yes he will."

"Got a cigarette?"

I reminded him there was a pack in his pocket.

He didn't feel his pocket. He seemed to be asking for the sake of a rainy day.

"I feel like traveling on," he said. The door fell shut behind him, locking me up with the silence. I watched Johnny walk away, taking quick, short steps, swinging his left arm wildly out to the side, and bringing his right arm up occasionally to pinch his nose. And then I watched the spot where he faded from, feeling lonely.

What the sun hides is the sound of the termites' teeth. The aria of the locust. The dry earth cracking open. Rotting stomachs. Crying farmers who have wasted prayers. The sleep disorders of advertising executives. The sun makes you mistake the neurotic tics of businessmen for smiles. It hides the agony on the faces of those who exchange pleasantries in corporate bathrooms during breaks from cubicles. The sun hides the cracking earth. It hides the drought. It hides the heat.

The motel man came in, poured a cup of coffee and sauntered back up the center aisle, smiling a strange half-smile discernible only from the changing shape of his beard. The beard then closed squarely again over his mouth as he faced me from across the counter. He sipped his coffee and lifted his tired eyes.

"You got it made back there, don't you?"

"It's alright," I said.

"We run like madmen searching out rest, said Rimbaud," he said.

I nodded.

"Name's Paul," he said.

"Leo Gray."

"Glad to know you, Leo. Glad to know you." He pulled on the end of his beard and then reached for a tabloid he took with him to the end of the counter, where he spread it open, flipping pages and sipping coffee, pulling on his beard.

"Jesus is scheduled to visit Earth October the 21st."

"Let me know if you see him coming," I said.

"Will do," he said.

I stared out the window, and Paul read his tabloid and we let the silence fall between us.

A very old and disoriented man stepped stoop-shouldered through the door. He stepped inside and stopped, patting the pockets of his pajamas. A large bandage was taped to the inside of his left arm. I looked at Paul, who simply raised his eyebrows and went back to his tabloid.

"Good morning," I told the man.

He shuffled closer to the counter, looked up at me. Said, "I just got out of the hospital." He raised his left arm and showed me his plastic bracelet. His face resembled that of a small girl pouting. A thin layer of white hair stood up on his head.

"I've got eleven dollars," he said, "but it's back at the hospital. You give me a beer and I'll bring you some money first thing in the morning. And I'm not just saying that. I'm a man of my word." He stared at me deeply then, showing me his word.

"Help yourself," I said. I pointed to the beer cooler, and the man shuffled that way, nodding to Paul as soon as he crossed his line of vision. Paul nodded back, flipped a page.

The old man stood before the beer cooler, trying to make a choice. He looked over his shoulder at me, said, "are all these beers about the same temperature? I want the coldest one."

"They're all about the same," I said.

He took one out and walked back to the counter, trying to twist off the cap.

"All my strength is gone," he said. "You got a opener?"

I took the beer, twisted off the cap. Pulled a Styrofoam cup from under the counter, poured the beer into the cup, threw away the bottle and handed the man the cup. "In case of cops," I said.

"I appreciate it," the man said. He sipped from the cup and sighed with great relief.

"Apocalyptic drought is in full bloom," Paul said.

The old man nodded in affirmation.

"I just got out of the hospital," he said again. He rubbed his chest and stomach to show me the areas where he must be sick. "It's the cancer," he said, "but I don't tell many people that. Most folks act like it's contagious. I'm still supposed to be in the hospital, but they can't do nothing for me. I tried to go home, to my apartment, but the locks has been changed. Somebody else is in there now. I guess I didn't know how long I've been away. My name's W.B. Newman. I'm Paul Newman's cousin."

"Leo Gray," I said, and I stuck my hand out for shaking. W.B. gripped it weakly and held on. "That's Paul."

Paul looked up from his tabloid and said hello. W.B. raised his Styrofoam cup, and said, "pleased to know you." He turned back to me, holding his stomach.

"I went by the Salvation Army to see if they had a cot, you know, but they said they was full up. I never would've thought it. I guess you never hear much around here about folks like me needing a place to stay. You know?"

I nodded.

"I'm sixty-six years old," he said.

He sipped his beer and moved toward the door so he could look out at the night.

"My wife died eleven years ago in March," W.B. said. "My son's in California—in the computer business. I had this little place down on Prince Street where I was staying until I went into the hospital. All the people around there, they'd come by asking if they could borrow twenty dollars, and then they'd go off and come back in a little while with these things they'd put in their pipes to smoke. A lot of them was black and white couples living together, which I don't much believe in, but they acted like they really needed the money, so I helped them when I could."

He sipped from his cup and stared down into it.

Paul said, "Fourteen hundred pound man finds lost sandwich in belly button."

"My car got impounded," W.B. said. "Gonna cost me a hundred and sixty-five dollars to get it out. All my pain medicine is in the glove box. I was in the Air Force twenty years. Flew fighter planes in Korea and then Vietnam. You ever been there?"

I stared at the scars on the man's face until the question caught up with me. "No," I said. "Never have."

"They say the atom bombs we dropped on Japan killed 80,000 people, but they only killed 60,000." He stared at me with cold eyes, preparing himself for the moment when I might disagree, but I simply nodded, and looked back out the window.

Paul said, "Former world's strongest man, Paul Anderson, now a thousand pounds, can't get out of bed. Stuck in his bedroom, emergency personnel are preparing to remove the roof so they can airlift him to the hospital."

"Have you got a bathroom?" W.B. said.

"Around back," I said.

He left his cup on the counter and shuffled outside, sliding his paper slippers across the pavement.

Paul said, "You ever noticed the lonely eyes of Sasquatch?"

"Who?"

"Sasquatch. That man-beast creature that supposedly roams the woods in the Northwest, popping out occasionally for photo-ops."

"I don't guess I know him," I said.

"Doesn't matter."

I stared out the window into the night. The quality of blackness was especially rich and deep, uncorrupted by stars. I stared at the night until W.B. Newman walked back into the store, sighing. I handed him his cup of beer, but he waved it off.

"I can't keep anything down. I just vomited in your bathroom back there. I'm sorry about that."

"Don't worry about it," I said.

W.B. Newman faced the door and looked out into the night. I began to wonder whether the old man was running a scam. Then I felt guilty for thinking that. I'd already seen my share—high school kids who gave me fake rings to hold for collateral until they could get to a bank machine, men in polo shirts who wrote bad checks, and a series of others passing through on their way to Florida who shared sob stories about dead grandparents and empty stomachs and cheating spouses. But the eyes rarely matched the stories, and the mannerisms were too busy trying to sell themselves. Still, I never turned them down. Having to tell such desperate stories so late at night was enough. One sickness was just as real as another.

But W.B. Newman hadn't yet asked for anything. He was simply talking.

He turned from the door and looked at me. "Do you know who I am?" he said.

I leaned with one arm on the counter, and put my other hand on my waist. "You're W.B. Newman," I told him.

"Paul Newman is my second cousin."

I nodded. Paul flipped pages from his tabloid.

"We grew up together in Cleveland, Ohio. Did you see that last picture he did, where he played that old man who lived upstairs from the old woman who was always trying to get him to have some tea?"

"I don't guess I saw that," I said.

"That woman was my aunt—our aunt—me and Paul's. You know what she said to him in the end? She said, 'you've been good to me.'" He stared at me with the same intensity he'd used when talking of atom bombs.

I nodded.

Paul looked up from his tabloid. "What about *The Hustler*?" he said. "Did you teach him to play pool?"

"My brother did. My brother taught him everything he knows. All those trick shots and everything. My brother played against Fats Domino and my brother beat him. Sure as hell did." The intense eyes focused this time on Paul.

"You mean Minnesota Fats?" Paul said.

"That's right." And again the eyes. "That's right. Minnesota Fats. Played against him and beat him too. Sure as hell did."

And he looked back to me, eyes softened.

"If I were to give you forty dollars, would you get a motel room for the night? There's a motel across the street that Paul here manages. He'd put you up."

"Sure," Paul said. "I'd do it for thirty."

"I'll give you forty," I said. "That way you can get some breakfast if you need it."

His eyes moistened. "You must be an Air Force man," he said.

I opened the drawer and pulled out two twenties and passed them over.

"Shalom," he said. "You know what that means?"

I told him I didn't know.

"It means, 'God be with you.'"

"Shalom," I said.

"That's right." He turned his head toward the door and pointed. "That motel right there?"

I nodded.

"Looks better than the hospital," he said.

"Better than Palm Springs," Paul said. "I'll go check you in." He put his tabloid back in the rack, sighing. "Leo," he said, "give me a pack of cigarettes on my tab."

I tossed Paul a pack of cigarettes as he stepped toward the door. W.B. looked at me as he shuffled forward, nodding with moist eyes. They started across the parking lot, and the door closed behind them, locking in the silence. I watched them walk across the street and disappear behind a door. And then I looked above the door into the night and stared at the rich black sky. A high-pitched ringing pierced my inner ear and bounced along the basement of my brain. The ringing changed gears, and rubbed the backs of my eyes, and I felt awake. I felt more awake than I'd ever been. I felt the kind of bright lucidity that begs for feeding. My senses started burning. I felt myself floating out the window and into the night, and it scared me. I pulled down a random pack of cigarettes and smoked two in quick succession. I smoked to quell the burning. I lit a third, and went into the beer cooler and rapidly drank three beers. To quell the burning. I opened a fourth and took it, along with my empties, into the night. I gulped my last beer beside the dumpster as I looked into the night at the pointed edges of random stars. The smell of garbage swam inside my nostrils, but there lingered on my tongue the taste of stars. I could see every star, without seeing a single constellation, those named groups that reinforce a bias toward segregation. I inhaled the garbage and stared at stars.

What the sun hides, above all else, is mystery. The sun shines on the data showcased by the red-eyed computer scientist. But there is no mystery in fact. Information is not knowledge. The truth cannot be quoted. Where there is darkness and silence, there is uncertainty, and therefore life. Not knowing propels deep peace.

I threw my last beer into the dumpster and walked toward the first of the chores I needed to complete before Gladys came. I filled fifty bags of ice with three and a half scoops each, twisted black ties around the tops and gently placed each bag into a grocery cart I filled three times, bending and straightening until my back hurt and my hands grew numb with cold. Before emptying the first buggy, I took a shovel from the store and broke up blocks of ice inside the ice machine that had spilled from torn bags and formed clusters in the corners, ignored by countless workers before me. And then I neatly stacked new rows of ice, pushing my upper body into the cooler to pack the bags tightly, nestling them in grooves like properly stacked firewood. I returned the cart to the storeroom and went outside again, to the back of the building, where I bent and picked up a twenty-foot long wooden pole used for measuring gas. I lofted the pole over my shoulder and walked with it back around the front. The five a.m. air was perfect. Hot and calm and unburdened by the sun. Hot enough to settle on the skin and stick, while giving no trouble to the eyes. My eyes too were warm. The only sound in the world was the subtle buzzing of the lights above the tanks. I looked into the night and breathed, imagined myself floating in the warmth of an amniotic sac. Told myself I should remember this moment in history when I stood like this staring into the night and felt my eyes open.

I'd taken a pack of chewing tobacco from the store, deciding I needed to know the taste. Had seen the inflated cheeks of men from the paper mill, and understood now, that their passion for tobacco came from a desire to forget machines and taste the country. I inserted a wad, and quickly grew relaxed. Sucked nutrients from the earth and spit out its spirit. Sent streams of brown juice arcing through the night and felt the chemistry of my body reconstitute itself. Kneeled on the asphalt and removed the metal lids of the gas wells, placing two fingers in holes placed on opposite ends. The smell of gas stormed my nose and stirred something in my brain. I dipped my head inside the well and breathed deeply. Spit down into it and listened for the splash. Dropped the wooden stick down into the first tank and pulled it out again, putting a finger on the spot where the wetness stopped, which was somewhere between the thirty-two and thirty-three inch mark. Lowered the stick two more times to be exact. For Gladys. I wanted Gladys to have the most accurate reading possible. Except for my giving away the store, I wanted her to believe I would work well for her. I performed the same procedure with the other two tanks, put the metal lids back in place and returned the wooden pole to the back of the building where it belonged. Took readings then of the three gas tanks, registering on my clipboard the little numbers beneath the larger numbers and then double-checked them for accuracy. For Gladys. I wanted to do everything within my power to make Gladys live free of fear. Saved the bathrooms for last. Emptied and washed the mop bucket, using Clorox from the shelf. Rinsed the mop with scalding water and rang it tightly with both hands until my wrists burned. Swept the women's bathroom before mopping, filled a dustpan with loose dirt, paper towels, and a spent syringe. Scrubbed the sink with Comet, and sprayed the mirror with Windex, wiping twice. Emptied the trash and inserted new bags, tying them tightly at the lips of cans.

Smelled the men's bathroom before I saw the mess. A layer of shit had been spread against the back wall, and part of a single turd lay in the sink, which had been a painter's palette. A puddle of piss lay in the corner. I took two backward steps into the night to get a breath, and stared at the mess inside. It occurred to me not to clean it. It occurred to me to plead ignorance, and run away from it and leave it for someone else to do. But I knew that someone else would be Gladys, and I didn't want her to have to see it. To distract myself, I started singing. I sang fragments of the gospel hymns I remembered from Johnny and the mill worker. I sang bits from different songs and put them all together. I spat tobacco juice into the puddle of piss and then I mopped it up, singing swing down sweet chariot swing down stop and let me ride. I threw my mop against the wall and sang of gathering at a beautiful beautiful river. I spit into the sink and cleaned it out, singing of echoes coming from the burning bush on the far side banks of Jordan. I washed my mop under the outside spigot and twisted it tightly with my hands, singing of angels coming for to carry me home. I returned everything to its proper place, for Gladys, and went outside again to look into the night.

I cleaned the bathrooms every night. Every night, I measured the gas wells and read the pumps. I performed my routine of jobs each night with loyalty and perseverance. And pretty soon, the nights started wearing uniforms. I lost track of the names that people assign to days; found this knowledge as useless as the facts I once double-checked for articles. When I finished my routine of chores, I often went to the rear of the building and ascended the rusty ladder attached to its side. I walked across the roof and stood on the edge, and looked up into the night. I did this about a half-hour before first light, when the air was its softest and most forgiving. Warm fingers descended and lifted every hair on both my arms. The air smelled strongly of the paper mill, but it was as familiar now as it had been in my childhood, and was no longer offensive. The air crawled into my lungs and constructed nests. I looked into the blackness until the blackness blurred, and then I blinked and refocused on the blackness. There were no sounds except for the dim buzzing of the lights above the tanks. Except for the buzzing, there was nothing. There was only the blackness and the buzzing. I looked up into the night and often let my eyes wander over my neighborhood. My eyes floated outside my body and drifted into the night. They drifted over the motel and saw its lost occupants sleeping soundly. I saw Paul staring at the ceiling, fighting off dreams of foreign places. I drifted past the motel into the trailer park and saw Johnny sitting on concrete steps, sipping beer and smoking cigarettes. My eyes floated over the string of failed businesses and the shanties and shotgun shacks and the black iron fence that wound around the government housing, and they moved over all the tin roofs until they settled over my mother's house, dark like the rest, except for the blue light of a television bleeding through a bedroom window. I heard my mother's breathing coming out like cracked whistling, and I saw inside her dreams to the blisters on her fingers that came from separating scorpions from shrimp. I saw E.B. Miller's legless body buried in a grave, dust mounting in the corners of his mouth. I saw all the Pine trees from here to Maine give way to concrete. Then my eyes went to the ocean and rode dark waves to the shores of distant continents. I saw the putrid bathwater of England's royalty and I saw the bulldozed graves of countries annexed for the dollar. I saw celebrities throwing temper tantrums because movie screens weren't big enough. I saw the hollow eyes of beggars in Bangladesh. I saw the portrait of a bank president drying on the ceiling of the Vatican. I saw the broken spines of Chinese farmers. I saw newspaper publishers teaming with television and the Internet to keep the attention of the sick and dying, one company under God.com. I saw the sick and dying filling stadiums, lifting their arms toward a dancing messenger come to tell them they were sinners. I saw the devil behind the messenger, keeping time on drums. I stared at the blackness until my vision blurred, and then I blinked and refocused on the blackness. I saw myself back on the roof, growing old as I stared into the sky. I let the air build nests inside my lungs. I stood on the edge of the roof night after night, waiting for the time when I could wash myself inside a South Georgia thunderstorm. And when it came, I spread my arms and let it punish me. I threw back my head and let it pelt my face. I tasted the rust in rain. Coo-cooed the lightning. I tapped my foot to the baritone thud of thunder. I felt it kick my chest. I looked through the thunderstorm until I spotted the headlights that belonged to Gladys. And then I ran to her, childlike, ready to let the night pour out of me.

Matthew Deshe Cashion was born in North Wilkesboro, North Carolina, and grew up on St. Simon's Island, Georgia. He presently works at Mitchell Community College in North Carolina.